STEALING HIS HEART

AN ACCIDENTAL PREGNANCY ROMANCE
(IRRESISTIBLE BROTHERS 3)

SCARLETT KING

MICHELLE LOVE

CONTENTS

BLURB

The moment I saw that tempting spitfire I knew I was in trouble.
The way her petite little body called out to me,
All of my billions couldn't stop me from wanting her—needing
her.

Life on my ranch was simple before she came along,
Calm, ordered, boring even.
The moment we met, everything changed.
We spent every waking, passionate moment together.
I was lost in her.
Consumed by her.
But she's got it in her head this is just a fun little distraction.
I want more—I need all of her.
My desire to own her has pushed us to the breaking point,
And I'm about to lose her...forever.

I'll fight like hell to not only prove to her I'm the man she needs,
But the man that will protect her and our unborn baby.

CHAPTER ONE

Cash

Carthage, Texas—Panola County
  January 1ˢᵗ

As the snow fell, my heart pounded with each flake I witnessed falling to the ground along the side of the road. A grandfather I not only never had known but hadn't even heard of had left my brothers and me a ranch in a town a little over an hour away from where we'd lived. A suburb of Dallas was where we'd always called home; now I wasn't sure where we'd call home.

All I knew for sure was that Mom and Dad weren't on the attorney's list of the people who'd inherited Collin Gentry's things. Even though he was my father's father, the man had left everything he had to the three of us and no one else. Why? I didn't know.

Tyrell, the oldest of the three of us, was the one to get a phone call on Christmas day from the man who'd said he was Allen Samuels, our grandfather's lawyer. He'd set everything up and now we were in Carthage, Texas, about to see what he'd inherited. Our father thought it would be a real headache, but I had other ideas.

We'd ridden on a private plane from Dallas to Cartage's small municipal airport. From there, Allen came in a limo to pick us up. He sat in front of us, looking through a folder as we all sat quietly, waiting to hear what he had to say.

Finally, the lawyer put the folder down to look at us. "The whole of the estate, that includes Whisper Ranch, the thirty-thousand square foot home that's on the ranch, and of course all of the vehicles, including the Cessna Citation II you came in on, belongs to you three men now." Allen looked over his shoulder then tapped on the dark glass that separated us from the driver. I saw the window between the driver and us come down. "Davenport, we need to make a stop at Mr. Gentry's bank please."

With a nod, the driver said, "Sure thing."

Allen turned his attention to Tyrell. "Tyrell, what have you been told about your paternal grandparents?"

"Not much," my oldest brother said. "My mother's famous quote when any of us asked about our grandparents was that if one couldn't say anything nice about a person, they shouldn't say anything at all. We'd assumed our grandparents weren't very good people."

"Yeah, Mom and Dad didn't like even to be asked about any of them," my brother Jasper added. "So, we stopped asking when we were very young. Just asking them who our grandparents were put them in terrible moods."

The lawyer nodded. "I see." We pulled into the parking lot of the Bank of Carthage. "Here we are. I'm going to have you all put on the ranch's bank accounts. And we can transfer the remainder of your grandfather's money into accounts that you each will personally open with this bank. If that's okay with you. You certainly can open accounts elsewhere if you'd like to. Your grandparents used this bank exclusively for years. I can assure you that the president appreciates Whisper Ranch's business and does everything they can to keep their customers happy."

Tyrell shrugged as he looked at Jasper and me; we sat on either side of him. "This bank seems as good as any. What do you guys think?"

Thinking about what we should do, I ran my hand through my hair. "Sounds fine to me. It'll be my first bank account anyway." I'd always worked for cash and hadn't had any need for a bank account before. Now it seemed I would need one.

Jasper shrugged. "Sounds okay to me too. All I've got in my bank is about twenty bucks. Hell, I might not even have that. I bought a bottle of Jack before getting on the plane—that might've overdrawn my account, and I might owe the bank something."

"This bank will do for us, Allen," Tyrell said as we started getting out of the car. "Thanks. He said your name is Davenport, right?"

The driver held the car door open for us. "Yep. I also drive various tractors and trucks at the ranch too. You need a ride, you call me and I'll get you there."

Tyrell didn't look like he was comfortable with something as he asked, "If you don't mind me asking, what's your first name?"

"Buddy," the driver said. "Your grandfather liked to put on airs."

"We're not like that at all. Mind if we call you Buddy instead?" Tyrell asked.

Buddy seemed happy about that. "Not at all. It would be nice, actually."

Jasper clapped the man on the back. "Nice to meet you, Buddy. I'm Jasper, this is Tyrell, and the little feller there is Cash, the baby brother of the Gentry family."

None of us were little fellers, and I always took offense at how Jasper teased me about that. "Jasper, you're the littlest out of all of us, you jerk."

Flexing his left bicep while threading his fingers through his dark hair, Jasper replied, "By a smidgeon of an inch, Cash. You're shorter."

"Also by a smidgeon of an inch." I walked ahead of them. "This bank is pretty fancy."

"It's the best one in this little town," Allen said he stepped in front of me, opening the door. "Here we go. Mr. Johnson is the bank president. He'll be handling this for us."

"The *president* will handle all of this?" Tyrell asked, sounding surprised. It had me thinking that bank presidents didn't often handle things of this nature. "How much money are we talking about, Allen?"

The lawyer cocked his head to one side, looking a little confused. "Are you telling me that even with the jet, the mansion, and the ranch, you still don't understand how much money your grandfather was worth?"

"Not a clue," Jasper said as he came inside and looked around. "Whoa. Posh."

Tyrell came in and looked up at the chandelier in the middle of the ceiling. "I haven't seen many banks with a thing like that hanging above peoples' heads before."

Everyone in the bank looked at us as the lawyer led us to the back of the large, open area. "This bank deals with a lot of exclusive businesses here in Carthage. They can afford certain luxuries that other banks cannot."

"Hello, gentlemen," a young woman said as we came into a small office. "You must be the Gentrys."

My oldest brother introduced himself as he shook her hand. "Tyrell."

Jasper nodded. "Jasper."

A smile went clear across her face—and a pretty decent face it was, too. "Then you must be Cash."

"Yep." I shook her hand as I smiled back at her. "And you are?"

"Sandra, the bank president's personal assistant." She let go of my hand, still smiling away. "And if you gentlemen will follow me, I'll let Mr. Johnson get things started." Her attention turned to Tyrell. "By the blue jeans and T-shirts, I assume you'll will be greatly surprised by what you're about to inherit."

Dad had told us that we'd most likely inherit only enough money to pay off our grandfather's debts. I didn't have hope for much more than that. But the way the lawyer and secretary acted told me our parents might not have been right about things after all.

As Sandra ushered us in, the bank president got up, greeting us warmly. "Bryce Johnson at your service, gentlemen. Please take seats anywhere you'd like. Can I offer you a cigar? They're Cuban. Or a drink perhaps? I've got a thirty-year-old scotch that would be perfect for this occasion."

As we sat down, Tyrell answered for all of us. "Okay, Bryce. We're pretty sure this ranch is swimming in debt. And we're not even close to being ranchers. Our father's advice was to find a buyer for it and move on."

I didn't see why my oldest brother needed to rush through anything. Narrowing my eyes at him, I let him know what I wanted. "I'd *love* a scotch, Tyrell. Let the man handle this meeting, will ya?"

"Scotch for everyone then," the bank president told Sandra, who left to get the drinks. "So, Allen hasn't filled you all in on things?"

"I have," the lawyer said. "Not the exact numbers, but I've told them about everything they now own. They don't seem to get it, Bryce."

Sandra came back with our drinks. "Here you go, gentlemen. Enjoy." Offering us each a crystal glass of expensive scotch, she gave me another smile. I was used to the attention. Most women did pay special attention to me. I credited my shoulder-length dark waves for most of the attention; my blue eyes didn't hurt either.

"A hell of a lot of hoopla, don't ya think?" Tyrell asked just before taking a drink.

Sandra winked at me. "You're all worth it." She put the tray down on a nearby table then took a seat on a chair nearest to me.

The bank president gave us each a piece of paper with some numbers on them. "I'll let the numbers speak for themselves."

"Not sure how to say this number," Tyrell said, sounding confused. "And not sure I understand what it even means. Our father told us there has to be debt that the ranch has built up."

The banker laughed as if that was the craziest thing he'd ever heard. "Whisper Ranch is one of the most profitable businesses this bank deals with. What you each are looking at is your third of the money Collin Gentry had in his personal accounts." He handed a paper to Tyrell. "This is what's in the ranch account."

Still wearing a confused expression, Tyrell said, "If I'm seeing this right, the ranch is worth millions."

"You're not seeing it right," the banker said. "Look again."

My oldest brother didn't seem to get it. "Oh, thousands."

Unlike Tyrell, I did understand the numbers on all the pages we'd been handed. "Tyrell, the ranch is worth *billions*, and we've each inherited fifteen *billion* dollars."

Still, my brother wasn't convinced as he said, "Dad said there'd be more money to pay out than we'd get."

The bank president set Tyrell straight. "Your father was wrong. Your grandfather went from only raising cattle to raising racehorses. You might've heard of some of his famous horses. The General's Son? Old Faithful? Coy's Burden?"

"We've never followed horse racing, sir," Jasper said. "I guess those are horses on the ranch?"

"They are," the banker said. "And they all are prize-winning stallions. Your grandfather began selling their semen and making a killing from it. Those sales, the cattle, and the racehorses have made him a pretty penny. Pennies that now belong to you three."

"Our father isn't mentioned at all in the will?" Tyrell asked.

The attorney took that question, which I wanted an answer to as well. "Look, I know it's difficult to understand but let me show you in writing why that is." He handed Tyrell another piece of paper. "See, your father signed this paper, stating that he wanted nothing from Collin or Fiona Gentry from that date forward. He wasn't forced to sign it. Coy did it to prove a point to his parents when they refused to acknowledge his marriage to Lila Stevens."

Tyrell looked as confused as I felt. "Wait. What?"

"See, your grandparents wanted to make the Gentry name something akin to royalty around here," the banker told us. "But your father fell in love with a girl from the wrong side of the tracks. A girl whose family lived on welfare. A girl who'd once worked as a maid at the ranch house."

We all looked confused as Tyrell asked, "Why would they never tell us about that?"

"Most likely because they didn't want you three to know what they'd walked away from," the lawyer said. "They chose love over money *and* their families. Your mother's family was just as against their marriage as the Gentrys were."

"Wow, seems our parents hid a hell of a lot from us." Tyrell looked at Jasper and me as we all felt shell-shocked by the news.

The lawyer wasn't done talking yet as he went on. "There's one more thing you need to know about the will, gentlemen. It stipulates that neither your mother nor father are ever allowed on the property. And your grandfather's money can never benefit them in any way. If you do so much as hand your parents five dollars, the entire estate, that includes the money, will revert to the state of Texas."

I thought that to be a bit much. "Harsh."

"Yeah," the bank president agreed. "Your grandfather was considered to be a harsh man. So harsh, most people think your grandmother died at the age of forty-five, only two years after your father left the ranch, because of his hard ways."

Who the hell am I related to?

CHAPTER TWO

Bobbi Jo

"Yeah, pull two cases of Crown out of the back and some Jack Daniels too." I walked around the bar to take stock of the beer in the cooler. "And five cases of Michelob Ultra. That's our best seller." Joey was new to the bar, and I knew I'd have to hold his hand for a while. "Once you've got those things up here and put away, you can go out to the parking lot and make sure it's clean. You know, no cigarette butts, no trash, nothing but a sparkling clean area for our patrons to park in."

His dark eyes met mine as he smiled crookedly. "And what is it that *you* do, Bobbi Jo?"

"Really newbie?" I put my hand on my hip. "You've been here all of five minutes and already you're sassing me?"

"Sorry," he said as he turned tail and went to the stockroom in the back of the bar. "I'll get that done. Am I gonna get to make some drinks tonight?"

"Hell yes." I planned to sit back and watch the new bartender do all the work. "I'll be supervising tonight."

The smile he wore told me Joey was okay with working all night.

And I was glad he was. It had been several years of me working by myself mostly. Finally, the owners of The Watering Hole had taken my advice—or better said—pleas for help.

While Joey did the hard part, I tidied up a bit then played a few hands of poker on my cell. Friday afternoons were usually hectic for me, but not this one. I was chilled out completely when the first guests walked through the front door. "Evening, folks."

The man and woman weren't locals and looked around the empty establishment. "Um, are we early?" the man asked as he put his arm around the lady at his side.

"You are." I took the chance to help them out, leading them to a nice table for two near the bar. "I've got a table with your name on it over here. I'm Bobbi Jo, your hostess for this evening."

The couple took the seats, both smiling and seeming a lot more relaxed as the man said, "For a moment there, I thought we'd stumbled into one of those private bars where only members are allowed."

"Not here at The Watering Hole. We welcome everyone." I pointed at the chalkboard behind the bar. "Those are our signature cocktails. Of course, we serve every beer known to man. And if you're a teetotaler, we have sweet tea, a variety of cokes, and even coffee."

"How about something to snack on?" the woman asked.

I offered our most ordered snack. "How about some saltine crackers with summer sausage and cheddar cheese on them?"

"Sounds great," the man said. "We'll have a couple of beers—whatever you've got on tap will be fine—and that cracker thingy too. She's starving."

"Coming up." I went behind the bar to make the tray of snacks before filling icy mugs with the beer. Joey came out with a couple of cases of beer to refill the backup fridge. "I've got this table, but we're about to get busy. Around here, if people drive by and there's even one vehicle in the parking lot, they tend to stop."

Putting the bottles in the fridge, Joey responded, "Ready, boss."

"Good. I like being called boss." Putting the things on a tray, I carried them to the table just as more people came inside. "Looks like you guys are the party starters this Friday. I'll check on you in a bit.

And if you don't feel like getting up, just raise a hand and I'll make sure a couple more beers get to you."

"Thanks," the lady said as she dug into the snacks. "I'm famished."

Famished wasn't a word often said in our little east Texas town. "Cool. Enjoy." People from out of town were always easy to spot.

The regular customers came in. Every one of them looked at the new guy behind the bar then at me. I just waved and smiled as they took their usual seats. Giving a quick glance at Joey, I cut my eyes to the tables where he'd need to get to in a hurry.

Taking my cue, he hauled ass to our best customers, and I knew then I really could sit back and watch him work. After putting some good music on the jukebox, I took out my cell and went to take a seat behind the bar. Tonight, I would oversee the cash register to make sure Joey knew how to use it and make change.

My feet propped on a barstool, I sat on another one, playing a game as more and more people came in. Joey was moving like lightning around the bar and I loved it. He went to the register to ring up a table, and I took the time to let him know how good he was doing. "Hey, you might just work out, kid."

"Thanks," he said, then took off again.

Sighing with relief that my hard days of working alone were over, I saw the door open again. This time three hunky guys came in. All tall. All ridiculously hot. All built like brick shit houses.

Joey hauled ass to the bar as the three men came toward it. "Uh, let me get them, Joey."

With a grin, he nodded. "Got ya, boss."

I gave the newcomers my full attention. "Hi. Welcome to The Watering Hole. You guys aren't from here, or I'd know what to pour you."

They took seats at the bar. Two of them looked around the crowded room while one looked only at me. His teeth, straight and white, glistened under the blue neon lights of the bar. "We like beer and plenty of it," he said.

By their magnificent physiques, I knew their brand of choice.

"Three Ultras then." I grabbed frosted mugs from the freezer then filled them with the cold beer we kept on tap. Putting the drinks on the bar in front of them, I gave them a bit of southern hospitality. "On the house. It's not often we get newcomers in here."

One of them looked right into my eyes. His blue eyes matched those of the other two men. "Get ready to see us around. We're going to be living here now. We're the Gentry brothers. I'm Tyrell, this guy here next to me is Jasper, and that little guy on the end is our baby brother Cash."

The guy on the end was anything but little. "Nice to meet you, boys. I'm Bobbi Jo. And I'm very nosy. So don't be offended when I ask you lots of personal shit, 'kay?"

The guy on the end, Cash, nodded as he took a drink of his beer. "Keep my mug filled, and you can ask me anything you want, beautiful."

Filling a bowl with fresh peanuts, I put it in front of the men as I looked into the baby blue eyes of Cash, trying not to salivate over his dark waves of thick hair that hung to his broad shoulders. "Okay, for starters, how about you tell me what made you move to our little town of Carthage?"

The one who'd been introduced as Jasper answered my question. "We've inherited the Whisper Ranch."

"Gentry is what you said your last name is?" I mused. "So, you're related to old man Gentry—the rancher who rarely left home. Wow, I didn't know that man had any family."

Cash grinned at me. "Yeah, we've been told he was a hard ass. Not that we knew him or even of him. Our father didn't want anything to do with his father."

Tyrell asked, "Do you know how many people or who attended Collin Gentry's funeral?"

I had no idea at all. "I'm not into the whole obituary scene. I know a lot of town gossip though. You don't want me to tell you what kind of things I've heard about Collin Gentry though; I promise you that."

Tyrell looked at the pool tables then back at Jasper. "Care to let me beat you at pool?"

"I'll let you try." He got up, and the two of them left, leaving handsome Cash behind.

"So, you guys are living at the ranch then?" I asked as I picked up a glass and a white bar towel to clean it. It was a habit that I had.

Nodding, he took another drink. "That house is huge. I'd never seen a log cabin mansion before, and now I'm gonna live in one."

I'd never seen nor heard of the house on Whisper Ranch. "I bet it's awesome."

"You'd bet right." The way he smiled made my heart skip a beat—and my heart didn't do shit like that. "So what do you do, besides tending bar here at The Watering Hole?"

"Sleep mostly," I said with a laugh. "This is my job, my leisure activity, and most of the time, my social scene as well."

"You don't get out much is what you're saying?" He chuckled, making his chest move, taking my attention.

Mesmerized by the man, I answered, "If you ever want to find me, your safest bet is looking right here."

"Cool." He took another drink. "It's always nice to know where I can find a pretty girl to talk to. Care to hit me again, beautiful?"

Going to get him another frosted mug, I bit my lower lip as I caught him giving my ass the once-over through the mirror behind the bar. Maybe he thought I was as hot as I thought he was.

As I filled the mug, I had to let him know he wasn't the first customer to come onto me. "You know, I've heard just about every pickup line there is. And 'beautiful' is a thing I'm called at least ten times each night. I would think a man of your total hotness would have better lines than what you've come up with so far."

"That sounds like a challenge." He took the mug from me, his fingers grazing the back of my hand as he did so. "So, how about if I don't try to pick you up at all then?"

The way my blood ran hot told me I wouldn't hate it if he tried to pick me up, but I wasn't that kind of girl who wore her heart on her sleeve. "That would be best, Cash. I'm not the dating type anyway. You'd be wasting your time."

"Yeah, I can tell." His lips curved into a sly smile. "You'd be wasting your time too, as I don't like to date either."

My bets were that he didn't have to date. Women probably just fell at his feet, and he took them any way he wanted to.

"Cool. Glad to see we're on the same page, stud."

CHAPTER THREE

Cash

The petite blonde behind the bar had a glow about her that took my attention completely. Not many women could do that for me. I wasn't that easy to attract, but she was doing it without even trying to. "Yeah, dating is a joke." I sipped my second beer.

"I agree." She ran a white towel over the already clean bar. "Why go out to eat with someone to see if you've got something in common? I mean, we all have to eat, right? Why see if you have that in common?"

"Well, there are different tastes in food," I argued. "Once, I hooked up with this chick, and we went back to her place. She had a fridge full of nothing but cans of tuna fish. I thought she must've had a cat that I hadn't seen yet."

"Oh, hell," Bobbi Jo said with a wince. "Bet she didn't."

I nodded. "Yeah, she didn't have a cat. What she did have was a strict diet of canned tuna. Needless to say, I didn't stick around that night to see what that kind of diet had done for her."

"I bet it had done a number of things for her." She held her nose.

"Including giving her that fresh out of the can scent in her nether regions."

"Yeah, that's what I assumed too." I ate a peanut that she'd put out fresh for us. "I didn't want to find out firsthand."

"Smart." Moving to the register, she picked up a pen and a piece of paper. "Tonight, you and your brothers are on the house. That's how we welcome new residents of Carthage around here. And, of course, we hope you'll come back to visit us often enough to make up for the treat."

"Of course." I already had a good idea that I would love frequenting the fine establishment. "We're from Dallas. I can't say this is the nicest or worst bar I've ever been in, but I can say that the bartender is quite charming."

She looked behind her at the guy taking a bottle of Crown off the shelf. "You talking about Joey?"

The guy looked at me, wiggling his dark brows. "Hey there, mister."

"Hi there, Joey. Name's Cash Gentry." I gave him a nod.

He stopped as he looked at me. "Gentry?"

"Yep." I took another peanut.

"Like the Whisper Ranch Gentry?" he asked.

"Yep." I had the feeling we could expect a lot of that. "You've heard of the ranch?"

"My uncle has the ranch on the west side of that one. The Castle Ranch," Joey let me know. "His name is Richard. He's a good guy. He's about the same age as your grandfather was. He told me they'd gone to school together."

"Cool." Maybe I'd drop in and say hello sometime. It might be nice to know more about my grandfather.

"The Seven Pesos ranch is on the other side if Whisper Ranch," Bobbi Jo said. "George and Lori Sandoval own it. Well, Lori now. George passed away last year. He was your grandfather's age too. George went last year; your grandfather went this year." She looked at Joey. "Hope your uncle keeps himself in better shape than those two did."

Joey shook his head as he walked away to take care of other customers. "Me too. My cousins will make lousy ranch owners. They're snotty pricks who go to college in Lubbock."

Bobbi Jo looked back at me. "You look like you're college age. You going to school anywhere?"

"No." I wasn't ever planning on going to college. "My parents didn't have enough money for any of us to go to college. And none of us made good enough grades to get scholarships. But now, I don't see why we'd need to go get some degree. We're rolling in the dough."

"Yeah, I can see that." She gestured to my old shirt and blue jeans. "You look like a billion bucks."

Running my hand over my T-shirt, I said, "We just got the money today, honey. There hasn't been time to shop. But the next time you see me, I'll be looking like I'm worth my weight in gold."

Winking, she teased me, "Isn't horse semen a different color than gold, Cash?"

"So you know Whisper Ranch has made its money in the horse semen market." I had to hand it to the girl; she did know the town well.

"Racehorse semen," she corrected me. "More than one buyer has come to have drinks here, I'm proud to say."

"I figure all my brothers and I have to do is sit back and let the bucks keep rolling in." I hadn't had time to think about it much, but why bother with finding something to do if you had money coming in hand over fist already?

The slightest frown on her pretty face made me wonder what she thought about that.

"I hope you don't become *that* kind of man, Cash."

"What kind is that?" I had a feeling I knew but wanted to hear it come from her.

"A trust-fund brat." She ran the cloth over the bar again and then I could tell that she would soon become bored with me if I were nothing more than that.

"So, what would you have me do?" I had no idea why I'd asked her that.

"Something," she said. "Anything. Just don't sit back and drink your days and nights way while chasing loose women. Be something. Do something. Don't let this money go to waste. You know what I'm saying?"

"It sounds like you think I should—dare I say it?—work?" I'd barely gotten stinking rich and already the first woman I'd met after getting that way wanted me to work. "See, that's why I don't date or have serious relationships."

She seemed puzzled. "Because a woman would expect more out of you? Shallow man. I didn't see that coming."

"You're not typical, Bobbi Jo." I took a long drink of the beer as I watched her out of the corner of my eye.

"I try not to be." She pulled her jacket off, revealing tight and toned arms. "See, I'm a lot more like you than you think, Cash. I don't like relationships either. I think they stifle people." She flexed one bicep. "I like to work out when I'm not working. I've got my own gym in the garage at home. Men don't like women who are stronger or tougher than they are."

"You are absolutely right." I winked at her. "How about a refill, doll?"

With a heavy sigh, she got me a refill then slid it to me. "See, the thing is, I don't care if men don't like me."

"Because you like girls?" I teased her. I didn't see her as that type.

"You're a riot." She snapped the bar towel at me, catching me on the wrist. "I enjoy the company of men—just not for extended periods of time."

"So, you're a confirmed bachelorette then?" I asked as I'd considered myself a confirmed bachelor since puberty.

"Confirmed?" She tapped her chin. "I guess you could say that. I've got no intention of finding Mr. Right and making babies, taking care of a house, and driving a minivan. But having a little fun isn't a thing I'm against."

"Me neither." I held up my mug. "To you, Bobbi Jo, a woman who knows what she wants and isn't afraid of what anyone thinks about that." I had to respect that about the girl.

A blush covered her cheeks for only a moment as she ran her hand through her blond ponytail. "I guess I am coming off kind of strong. I'm not a man-hater by any means. "

"Nor am I a woman-hater." But I wasn't looking for anything serious. "I'm glad you and I have put ourselves out there. I don't like to guess what a woman wants. I bet you don't like to guess what a man wants either."

"What's to guess?" she asked. "Men want simple things. A woman who will dote on him, cook for him, care for him, give him what he wants, when he wants it. I'm just not into giving anyone what they want when they want it."

"Hey, how about another round over here, Bobbi Jo?" a guy called out.

Nodding, she went to grab some more beers for the table. "Maybe it's my job of having to give people what they want when they want it that makes me the way I am."

"Who knows for sure?" I took another drink as I watched her. The way her tight little ass moved when she hurried to give the beers to the table of men took my attention. It was a great ass after all. And her tits were pretty perky and plump too. She had that cute little hourglass figure that most women only dream of having.

When she came back behind the bar, I heard her stomach growl. "Oh, crap. I've gotta call in something for dinner. If I don't eat three times a day, I get extremely moody. How about you, Cash?"

"How about me what?" I had no idea what she meant.

"Have you eaten dinner yet?" I thought she was sweet for asking.

"I did. We have a home chef. He's the best. He made chicken fried steaks, mashed potatoes, and green beans. It was the bomb. Better than I've ever had before." Even recalling the meal had my mouth watering.

"Damn. That sounds good." She pulled her cell out of the pocket of her blue jeans. "Maybe you bring me your leftovers from time to time, and I'll treat you to free drinks. For now, though, it's the Dairy King to the rescue."

"I'll make that deal with you." It didn't matter that I had more money than I'd ever imagined. If anyone wanted to trade food for alcohol, I was in. "Any requests? I think I can get him to cook whatever I want."

"I bet you can, seeing as you and your brothers are his new bosses." She texted her order to the place she'd spoken about. "For the record, I love steaks. All kinds of steaks. And I like them rare."

"Me too." I liked that about her. "People who overcook their steaks piss me off. I'm like, a cow died for you, bitch. Don't ruin what it gave you."

Her laughter sounded musical, and I couldn't help the smile that took over my face. "I've literally said that before. My cousin Gina and I went to this steakhouse once, and she ordered her steak well done. I was like, why would you ruin your steak? That cow died for us."

"Seems we think alike." I hadn't ever had a girl who was just my friend. I'd never liked any girl that much. But Bobbi Jo wasn't like any girl I'd ever known. Most of them were so worried about attracting me that they watched every word that came out of their mouths.

"I highly doubt that." She jerked her head at some girls who came in the door. "I bet you and I are thinking totally different things about those girls there."

Looking at them, and seeing them look back at me, I nodded politely. "I see four young women who work together at what I'd bet is a bank." The fact was, I'd seen them at the bank we'd been at earlier when our lives were forever changed.

"Did the nametags clue you in?" Bobbi Jo asked, then laughed. "Too easy, Cash. Way too easy."

Yeah, just like being with you is.

CHAPTER FOUR

Bobbi Jo

The Gentry brothers had stayed until closing time at the bar the night before, and I'd had plenty of time to get to know at least one of them. Cash sat at the bar the whole night talking to me. He was entertaining, to say the least. And I knew I was the envy of all the girls in the bar, as the other ladies' eyes kept moving to look at the man who seemed to only notice me.

Sitting up in bed, I stretched as the noon hour had me waking up. Betty Sue sat at the vanity, painting on her face for the day. "You finally up, lazy bones?"

I nodded. "I wouldn't call myself lazy. I didn't get to sleep until nearly four in the morning. I've only slept the normal eight hours." She had the curling iron on, so I knew she was heading out later. "And where are you off to today?"

"Lance is taking me to Dallas. We're spending the night in a hotel." She blew a kiss at her reflection in the mirror. I thought it funny how much she adored herself. She and I were identical twins; we looked exactly alike. I didn't think of myself as God's gift to humanity, but Betty Sue sure did.

"Lance?" That was the first I'd heard of this guy.

"Lance Strongbow." She raised her perfectly arched brows. "He's Native American—Apache, I think."

"Really?" I had my doubts about that. My sister was so easily duped it wasn't even funny. "What color is his hair?" I had to ask that because once she fell for this guy who said he was Chinese. The only problem with that was he had blonde hair, blue eyes, a height of six-one, and the build of a Viking.

Guys lied to my sister about their native origins because she started off conversations with a tagline about hating Americans. I don't know if she thought it hip to hate herself and the people of her country or what, but she almost always started conversations with new people with that stupid line.

"Black," she said with a matter-of-fact expression on her painted face. "Long, shiny, black hair that hangs to his waist. This guy is the real deal. His grandfather's name is Trotting Horse. Now that's a real Native American name if you ask me."

I'd never heard a name like that, so who was I to argue with her about it? "So, you're going to Dallas with this guy? How well do you know him? You've never talked about him before." My sister had no sense of self-preservation; one had to ask her what the hell she thought she was doing most of the time. "And does Dad know about your little overnight date?"

"How old are we, Bobbi Jo?" She looked at me through the mirror.

"Twenty-two." In my opinion, that was old enough for some but not her. "But we live under Dad's roof, and you know his rules."

"What Dad doesn't know won't hurt him." She turned around to face me, then stuck her tongue out. "You won't tell on me."

She knew I wouldn't tell on her. But that was only because at least I would know where she was if she didn't show back up after one of her dates with strangers. "I won't tell. But I want you to send me a text of where you are once you get to where you're going. Plus, I'd like to know where he plans on taking you before you even leave town. I want to be sure he takes you where he says he will. And—"

She held up a hand to stop me. "Okay, okay, I know the drill, mother hen. I don't think there's anything to worry about. And, if you must know, I like the sense of danger that surrounds these men I don't know. Not knowing where they're taking me is part of the rush."

Rubbing my temples, I really thought that one day my twin would actually kill me. Not physically kill me, but mentally kill me. "Betty Sue, you shouldn't think that way."

"You wouldn't understand since you're a prude who never gets laid. Although you could if you wanted to." She ran her hand in a circle around her face. "We do look alike, and I have no problem at all getting men to notice me and want me."

"I don't either. Only I am a bit pickier than you are," I said. "As a matter of fact, I had a gorgeous man sitting at the bar talking to me all night last night."

"But did you hit the sheets with him?" she asked, eyes wide.

"No." I wasn't like my sister. I had to have more of a connection with someone before I got into bed with them.

"What are you waiting for?" she asked with a grin. "Does a man have to propose marriage before you give him any?"

I wasn't even thinking about marriage. "Betty Sue, since you're always talking about yourself, you may not know this about me, but I'm not into making commitments. I hate to date. I hate to be part of a couple. And I hate having to think of someone else's feelings all the time."

Getting up, she went to the closet to pick out her outfit for the day. "I don't think of anyone's feelings, Bobbi Jo. I have my fun then get out. You don't have to become a couple to have sex and do some fun shit together."

"How sweet," I said as I rolled my eyes. "Aren't you just a living doll, Betty Sue?" I had no idea what guys saw in her. Shallow to the core, the girl was a walking, talking nightmare. "Love them and leave them" was her motto, although she never disclosed that information about herself until the date was over.

"So, enough about me," she said as she came out of the closet with a short dress. "Who is this guy you met last night? Is he from here?"

I pointed at the tiny article of clothing. "You know it's January, right? And there's snow on the ground too. That dress is more suited for summer, not the dead of winter."

"He'll keep me warm." She slipped it on over her bra and panties. "So, this guy is ...?" She waved at me to get me to say more.

"His name is Cash Gentry." I wasn't sure how much info I wanted to give her. "He and his brothers are new in town. They've just moved here from Dallas." I thought that was the basics and she didn't need to know more than that.

"How old is he?" She looked through the jewelry box for something to add to her little dress.

"About my age, I think." I sighed as I pictured him in my head and my mouth just said things all on its own. "His six-two, blue eyes, dark wavy hair that hangs to his broad shoulders, and he's quite possibly the hottest man I've ever laid my actual eyes on."

"Intriguing," Betty Sue said. "And you said he has brothers. Yes, I can see myself in one or more of their arms now. Are they all as hot as this guy?"

I nodded. "They are. I doubt they'll be single long. Even the one who talked to me all night had the eyes of every woman in the bar—even the ones who were with their own men."

"Sounds like you might have a man for once, Bobbi Jo. If he's so eligible, you had better latch onto him and don't let go. And I'm not just talking about the other females in town; I'm talking about me too."

Something came over me as my sister looked at herself in the full-length mirror. "You need to stay away from him, Betty Sue."

Turning to face me, she smiled. "Why is that? Do you plan on taking him off the market?"

"No." I never planned on taking anyone off the market, especially since I didn't care to be taken off it myself. "It's just that he's nice. And I think he trusts people—maybe too much. You'd chew him up and spit him out. I don't want to see that happen to him."

"Then don't watch." She placed her hands on her hips then shimmied around the room. "So, how does my ass look in this dress?"

"Well, the lower part is peeking out at me if that answers your question." I laid back down and looked at the ceiling. I didn't see the white-popcorn ceiling at all; I saw his face. Cash's strong chin, cheekbones, and chiseled lips filled my mind. His deep voice, throaty laugh, and flirtatious words echoed in my head.

A knock came to the bedroom door. "You girls up?" Dad asked.

I sat up as Betty Sue darted to the closet to get a coat to cover up her daring outfit. "Yes, Daddy."

Rolling my eyes, I never could figure out how our father fell for Betty Sue's act. "You can come in, Dad."

Opening the door, he peeked inside. "I'm about to go to the station. Your mom is already at the feed store. What're your plans, girls?"

"Work, as usual," I said as I looked at my sister to see what she'd come up with.

"Oh, Daddy, I'll be out of town this weekend. A friend from high school has invited me to go with her to Dallas." Betty Sue batted her long, fake eyelashes. "I think her little cousin is having a birthday party. He's turning five. It should be great fun. You know how much I love children."

Dad nodded. "Okay. You be careful and shoot your sister a text when you get where you're going like you always do, Betty Sue." He turned his attention to me. "And you be extra careful tonight at work. You've still got that baseball bat behind the bar, right?"

I'd never had to use the thing my father had given me when I first went to work at The Watering Hole. "It's still right where you put it, Dad. I don't think there's anything to worry about this weekend."

"Still, that's a bar you're working in, missy." He shook his long finger at me. "It would be nice if you'd think about getting a job more like the one your sister has."

Betty Sue smiled at me. "I could ask Miss Cherry if she'd put you on, Bobbi Jo."

While I admired people who worked where my sister did, I couldn't see myself doing it. "Thank you, Betty Sue, but no. I don't think I've got what it takes to work at a nursing home. I like serving drinks and talking to half-drunk people; it entertains me."

Shrugging, Betty Sue said, "I feel like the people I talk too are half-drunk most of the time too. Or maybe it's just the fact most of them have Alzheimer's."

I was pretty sure the Alzheimer's had more to do with that than anything else. "Nevertheless, I like my job. And I feel secure there too, Dad."

"You know how I am about my little girls," he said. "You be careful out there. Bye now." He closed the door as I looked at my sister as she went back into the closet to ditch the overcoat.

"He had no clue about you, Betty Sue." I had no idea how my father was so clueless where she was concerned. "He's more worried about *my* job than what *you* do most weekends. Weird."

"I'm just glad it works that way." She stepped into a pair of heels. "Have fun serving drinks, wench. I'll be out with my man for the weekend in fabulous Dallas."

I had high hopes the guy who'd entertained me before would come back in and do it again tonight too.

CHAPTER FIVE

Cash

Riding one of the horses up the north fence, I saw a Ford truck coming through the pasture on the other side of our fence. As it got closer, I read the sign on the side of the truck: Castle Ranch.

Stopping my horse as the truck pulled to a stop. I got off the horse and went to meet the man who got out.

"Morning," he called out as he came my way.

"Morning." I could tell by the man's age and the way he dressed that this was Richard Castle, the owner of the ranch. The guy at the bar had told me about him. "I think I met your nephew Joey at The Watering Hole last night. You must be Richard Castle." I extended my hand over the barbed-wire fence.

He shook my hand as he smiled. "And you must be one of Collin's grandsons."

"I'm the youngest, Cash. It's nice to meet you, Mr. Castle. Joey told me you knew my grandfather."

Nodding, he shoved his hands into the pockets of his coat. "He and I were the same age. Up until high school, we were pretty good friends. Then he just kind of went on his own. We never were close after that."

"Sorry to hear that." I shrugged. "Or maybe it wasn't so bad that he went his own way. From what I've been told, he was a hard ass, to put it nicely."

Nodding, he agreed. "Yes, Collin was at best a hard ass. But your grandmother wasn't a thing like him. Fiona was a treasure that your grandfather didn't take care of well enough."

"So, my grandmother wasn't as bad as he was?" I had no idea about her. No one had spoken about her at all.

"Fiona was one of Carthage's most upstanding citizens. She worked with many charities here in town. After your father left, she really dove into the community and the church too." His smile told me he'd actually liked my grandmother. "If she hadn't been married to that old cuss, I would've courted her myself."

"And what did your wife think about that?" I had to ask.

He rocked back on the heels of his boots. "I never got me one of those. I kind of pined after Fiona so much that I never did find the right woman for me. I tend to think that's because *she* was the right one for me. I did have a couple of sons out of wedlock though. They lived with their mother in upstate New York. And one day, they will inherit this ranch. It's a shame really."

"Wow." I didn't know what I'd stumbled upon here. "Did you spend much time with my grandmother?"

His smile told me he had. "There were more than a few stolen moments. Your grandfather left her alone most of the time. There was a mistress that took a lot of his time. Fiona banished her for a while. Then the woman came back to Carthage. Her family lives here. She still lives right there in town in the house your grandfather bought for her too. Poor Fiona had to live out the remainder of her years, knowing the woman her husband really loved lived in the same town she did."

"What an ass." I shook my head as I thought how horrible that had to have been for my grandmother. "But my grandmother wasn't exactly a saint. She did agree with our grandfather about my mother not being good enough for my father."

Narrowing his blue eyes, he cocked his head to one side. "What makes you think she agreed about that?"

"Well, because it happened." I thought she had to have agreed with our grandfather about something so big, since it caused my father to take my mother and leave town, never to come back or say another word to his parents.

"Maybe you should ask your parents about that whole thing," he said. "I wasn't privy to all the information on that. Fiona was tight-lipped at times, especially where her son and husband were concerned."

"We're going to go see them soon. I will ask about that." It was obvious that the man had loved my grandmother. "So, I won't tell anyone, but did you and she ever ... you know?"

He shook his head. "No. Not that I didn't try. But your grand-mother was a good woman—a Godfearing woman too. She wouldn't have done a thing against her marriage vows."

"She didn't live much longer after our father left home."

Richard looked angry as he said, "No, she didn't live much longer after that happened. I know she was heartbroken over your father's leav-ing, but she was heartbroken over the affair her husband was having as well. Collin didn't waste much time after Fiona's death either. He brought that classless bitch to this ranch before even a month's time had passed."

"That is messed up." That old man had lots of nerve and huge balls to have done such a thing. "I can't understand why he did what he did. All I know is that for some reason, he decided to leave us the ranch and his money. So, what did he leave that woman?"

"All I know is that she still lives in the same house Collin bought her, and she drives the Cadillac he bought her just before he died." He shook his head as if disgusted. "But that woman has never worked a day in her life, so I know he had to have left her some money too."

"Well, I gotta get back. It was nice meeting you, Mr. Castle." I shook his hand again. "Sorry you never got to really get to know my grandmother. You seem like a nice man. I'm sure you would've treated her a hell of a lot better than my grandfather ever did."

"I sure would've. Nice to meet you too, Cash." He went back to his truck but turned to look at me before getting in and waved. "Bye now."

As I climbed back up on the horse, I wondered what kind of life my poor grandmother had lived. It sounded horrible to me.

The rest of the day went by slowly. All I kept thinking about was getting back to that bar and seeing that pretty little bartender again. And as we sat at the dining room table that night, I recalled something Bobbi Jo had said to me.

Ella, our young maid, was refilling our tea glasses. "Hey, Ella, do you think you can make me a plate to go?"

She put her hand on her hip and cocked her head. "Why?"

"Because I want to take dinner to Bobbi Jo." I smiled at her. "So, do you think you could make up a plate nice and pretty for her?"

"Who is Bobbi Jo?" The young maid was full of questions, and I saw my older brother, Tyrell, grinning.

"She's the bartender at The Watering Hole," I said.

"That place is a dive. Why do you want to go there?" she asked. "And what kind of a woman is that for you, Cash? A bartender? Really? You can have any girl you want. She raised her hand and gestured to my brothers too. "Any of you could have any woman you wanted in this town. Even the married ones. So, why do you want to impress a bartender?"

"First of all, I don't even *want* a woman, Ella." I wasn't looking for a relationship. "I'm trying to be nice. This young lady works hard, and she has to eat fast food all the time. I'd like to bring her a home-cooked meal now and then. Plus, she'll give me free drinks if I bring her something to eat."

That didn't explain a thing to the young woman. "Cash, that makes no sense. Sure, I can see you wanting to give a girl something good to eat, but don't do it so you can have free drinks. And there are lots better places to find a girl to like than at a bar."

"I don't want to find a girl to like, Ella. You don't get it. And I don't expect you to." I looked to Tyrell for some help.

"Ella," Tyrell said, "Cash is what you would call a player."

"No," I hissed.

Tyrell and Jasper nodded as Tyrell said, "Yes, that is what you are. See, Ella, Cash doesn't want just one girl. He wants them all. So, even you have to be careful where he's concerned."

"She does not!" I looked at the girl who my brother clearly had eyes for. "I think you're cute as hell, Ella. But I don't shit where I eat."

"Gross!" She shook her head.

"I mean that I don't mess with women who I have to see every day." I ran my hand over my face. "So you don't have to worry about me. What you do need to do is go into the kitchen and make me a plate of this magnificent food to go. And please make it look good."

"So you can impress her?" she asked.

I wasn't into impressing anyone. "No. I just don't want it to look unappetizing."

"So, no red rose on the top of it?" She walked out of the room, laughing at her joke.

I looked at Tyrell. "It would be nice if you could get your girl in check, bro."

"She's not my girl, Cash." Tyrell shook his head.

"You've caught her up in your strong arms twice already since we moved in. I think she *is* your girl." I took a drink of the fresh sweet tea Ella had filled my glass with.

"And I think I've never seen you talk so long to a woman before without it ending in the sack," Jasper said as he cocked his head. "You and that bartender never stopped talking. And you didn't even get a goodnight kiss. What's up with that?"

"I didn't ask her for one." I could've gotten one if I wanted one.

"So, you going after that tonight?" Tyrell asked. "Is that why you're bringing her dinner? A little crawfish etouffee in exchange for some tongue action?"

"You are a child, Tyrell." I finished the last of my dinner. "And now if you gentlemen will excuse me, I'm off to hang out at the bar. Maybe I'll play some pool and make some new friends."

"If you can pull yourself away from that pretty little bartender," Jasper teased me.

"She's not so hard to pull myself away from." I got up then stopped and turned to look at them "And she's easy to talk to."

"And look at," Jasper said. "She got a sister?"

"Hell if I know." I turned to leave then stopped again as it hit me that Jasper had said Bobbi Jo was something to look at and it kinda pissed me off. "And I'll have you know that Bobbi Jo is much more than just a pretty face."

"She sure is," Tyrell said with a grin. "She's girlfriend material."

My brothers knew I didn't want a girlfriend. "Don't even joke about that. But I don't think I've got anything to worry about. She's like me in that department. She doesn't want a boyfriend either."

Jasper just laughed. "Yeah, who would want to be the girlfriend of a rich, young, good-looking guy? Certainly not a poor bartender."

"Who said she's poor?" I hadn't said that. "And what do I care how much money she has anyway. We all came from nothing."

Tyrell held his hands up, gesturing to the grand dining room. "Need I remind you that we might not have known it, but we came from this, not nothing. And you will have to watch out for gold diggers, Cash. We all will."

Could Bobbi Jo really be a gold digger?

CHAPTER SIX

Bobbi Jo

When the door opened, and Cash came walking in alone, I had this feeling he'd come to see me. And I didn't like that at all. "Hi," I said curtly, nodding. "Beer?"

He shook his head as he looked at the pool tables which were full already. "I thought I'd play a game of pool. Looks like everyone thought the same way I did."

Trixie from the Speedy Stop couldn't take her eyes off him, and I watched her get up from the table of girls she sat at. I didn't have much time to save the poor guy. "Why don't you take a seat at the bar while you wait?"

Eyeing the empty barstool in front of me, he looked like he didn't know what to do. "Are there any other bars with pool tables around here?"

Trixie was closing in, and I had to move fast, or he'd be her mark for the night. Cash didn't need that. "Not any as good as this one. And that's not saying much. Come on. Sit down. I'll mix you up a drink if you're not in the beer mood."

Again, he looked at the empty chair as if it had snakes crawling all over it. "I don't know."

There was no time left as the woman with four kids at home reached out for him. I grabbed his hand, pulling him along with me. "Come on, Cash. Have a drink. It's on the house."

"Hey! I had my eye on him." Trixie shouted as I got him away from her in the nick of time. Thankfully, there was so much other noise in the bar, Cash hadn't realized she was talking about him.

I pretended I didn't hear her either. "So, what're your favorite flavors, Cash?"

He took the seat I'd been offering him as I went around to the other side of the bar. "Depends on what we're talking about. My favorite flavor of cake is strawberry."

"Definitely on the lower scale with that." I reached for a bottle of banana-flavored vodka.

Nodding, he seemed to understand me. "Yeah, no one else in my family likes strawberry anything. And the only candy I like is chocolate."

I pulled out the large bar of dark chocolate and the grater from underneath the bar. "Is there any other kind?"

He shook his head. "Not as far as I'm concerned, there's not." He smiled at me as I took the jar of red maraschino cherries out of the mini fridge. "You know, I wasn't in the best of moods when I came in here."

I'd had that feeling. "No way!" I winked at him.

He just laughed. "Yeah. It showed, huh?"

Holding two of my fingers a small space apart, I said, "Just a little." Then I took out a bottle of vanilla rum. "That's why I'm making you something unique. If you like it, I'm going to call it the Cash Special. Only nine ninety-five."

He looked at what I was doing with interest now. "So what are you making there, Bobbi Jo?"

"First, you tell me what had you all grumpy." I got out the Kahlua and was ready to start building the drink.

He sighed, then looked down at the bar. "This whole having money thing is making life harder than it was."

"I can't see how." I had to laugh. "If it's that bothersome, send it my way. I'll deal with the hardship of being stinking rich to save you the trouble." I was kidding of course.

When his blue eyes met mine, I had the idea he thought I might say something of that nature. "Bobbi Jo, if me and my brothers didn't have any money, would you have treated us to free drinks last night?"

Standing straight up, I had the idea he thought I was after him and his money. "Cash, I give all newcomers—who are new citizens of Carthage—free drinks for one night. And this drink is on the house because I'm using you as a guinea pig. There is no other reason for it."

The way he cocked his head told me he wasn't sure about what I'd said. "My brothers and I were talking at dinner tonight. We talked about how gold diggers might come after us now."

Nodding, I knew he was right. "Yeah, you've got to really watch out for them." I nodded in the direction of Trixie. "See that woman over there?"

He looked back to see her then looked back at me. "The redhead with the toothy grin?"

"Yes, her." I poured the Kahlua into a tall glass. "She's got four kids—all from different men. Now all these men have one thing in common. Money. Not anywhere near what you and your brothers have, but lots of money. And she got pregnant on purpose to get a percentage of their money. And she spotted you quick and in a hurry. I think she must have rich-man radar or something. Not many people know you or your brothers, nor your financial situation. Weird, huh?"

"I'll say." Cash looked back at her, and she waved at him. He didn't wave back as he looked at me. "I think you're right about her. I still haven't bought any new clothes. This jacket is the same one I wore in high school, and so are these cowboy boots."

"I don't think you need to be in a bad mood about those kinds of people, Cash. You'll be able to spot them from a mile away once you get used to it." I poured the other liquors into the glass then topped it with whipped cream, a cherry, and some chocolate curls. "Here you go—the Cash Special." I watched as he took the straw I slid across the bar to him.

One sip led to one long drink, then he sighed. "Ah. It's delicious."

"So, we've got a new drink then." I quickly filled out a recipe card and put it in the book of originals. "I like to come up with something new every now and then."

He smiled as he sipped the drink. "I like being your guinea pig, Bobbi Jo. It's fun."

"Good. I like having someone around who's not afraid to take chances and try new things." I put everything away as he sipped on the drink while looking around the bar. "So, what did your chef make you for dinner tonight?"

"Shit!" Cash put his drink down then got up and ran out the door.

I stood there, watching him and wondering what I'd said to run him off. Another customer waved me down, and I went to take the table some more beers, as Joey was busy. When I got back to the bar, Cash was back in his seat, and a Styrofoam container was in front of him. "For me?"

He nodded as he picked his drink back up. "And it's good too."

Opening the top, a wave of heat came up to meet my face as I took a long sniff. "I love seafood."

"I bet you do." He reached into his pocket and pulled out a plastic fork. "Here ya go. Dig in."

"You really thought of it all, didn't ya?" I was impressed. And when I took a bite, I was in Heaven. "Oh, yeah. Free drinks for a week for this. It's amazing."

He sat there, watching me eat as he sipped on the drink I'd made him. "You know, it wouldn't be considered a date if you came to eat dinner at my place sometime. It would be considered an act of kindness, I think."

"I'd take that act of kindness any day." I thought about it. "Wait, any day that I'm off, which are Sundays and Mondays." I winked at him. "And I wouldn't consider it a date either, so you're safe there, lover boy."

"Tomorrow is Sunday," he pointed out.

I didn't know what to say to that. So I just looked at him.

"So, how about you give me your number, and I'll call you when I'm coming to pick you up?" he asked.

I pulled out my pen and wrote my number down on a napkin. "How about you give me a call, and I'll come out on my own. We don't want anyone to get the wrong idea about us."

"No, we don't." He took the napkin then pulled out his cell and put my number into his contacts. I felt my cell vibrate in my pocket and took it out. "Is this you?"

He nodded. "Yep. Now you've got my number too. Try your best not to make any midnight drunk calls to me. I'm only human, you know."

"Since I don't drink, that ought to be pretty easy for me." I held up the bottle of water I kept under the bar.

"You work at a bar. You make up your own drinks. But you don't drink?" He looked confused.

"I do taste now and then." I took another bite and hummed with how good it was. "I can't wait for tomorrow. I bet it's gonna be great."

"Me too." He couldn't pull the smile off his face. "I'm glad you're going to come over. The place is so big, and I kind of get lost in it sometimes. It might be nice to check it all out with you."

"I've never been to the ranch, Cash." I had no idea what he thought I could do to help him.

"No, I meant it might be cool to get lost with you." He leaned forward, his breath sweet and warm near my lips as I leaned in close too.

I rested my chin in the palm of my hand. "I do believe my drink has gotten to you, Cash Gentry."

"You think so?" His eyes scanned my whole face. "I like those tiny freckles you've got across the tops of your cheeks. I didn't see them before. I guess you gotta get real close to see them."

I liked him this way; he was sweet and adorable. "I think I'll bring another one of Cash's Specials along when I come tomorrow. They seem to agree with you."

"*You* agree with me, Bobbi Jo." He sat back and looked me up and down. "You don't even try to look good, do you?"

"Huh?" I didn't try to look crappy either.

"I mean, you look good without trying to." He smiled sheepishly.

"Yeah, you're drunk. How about a coffee?" I went to pour him a cup.

"I'm not drunk," he protested. "I'm just pointing out a fact. You look like you just roll out of bed and put anything on and it works for you."

"I do a little more than just that." I put the cup of coffee in front of him. "But thank you?" I wasn't sure if he was complimenting me or not.

"You're welcome." He didn't argue about the coffee as he took a sip. "You even make great coffee, Bobbi Jo. Do you have any faults at all?"

My sister came through the door in her little dress, a tall man at her side, and her eyes on the man who sat in front of me. She left the man in the dust as she came straight to Cash's side. "Hi."

He looked at her, then at me, then at her again. "Has anyone ever told you that you look a hell of a lot like the bartender at The Watering Hole?"

She and I laughed, but I wasn't laughing with ease as she put her arm around Cash's shoulders and grinned at me in a way that made me extremely nervous.

CHAPTER SEVEN

Cash

With a woman hanging on my shoulder who looked a hell of a lot like the one who'd stolen my attention since I first laid eyes on her, I wondered why she wore so damn much makeup. "You know you could do without all that goop on your face, right?"

"Goop?" Her dark blonde brows arched as she looked at Bobbi Jo. "So this is him?"

"Who?" I asked as I looked back at the woman who hung all over me even though she'd come in with a man. A man who stood perfectly still, staring a hole in me.

Bobbi Jo just shook her head. "No. Would you mind getting off my customer, Betty Sue?"

"Betty Sue?" I asked. "Are you two twins?"

"What tipped you off?" the woman I now knew was named Betty Sue asked me with a grin.

"I'm a little tipsy, but I ain't drunk. I can see the similarities." I didn't know why I kept thinking about all the makeup the girl had on, but I did. "Why do you have so much shit on your face, Betty Sue?

Look at your sister." I pointed at Bobbi Jo's face. "She's beautiful naturally. You could look like that too."

Grimacing, Betty Sue said, "I like to wear makeup. I feel prettier with some on."

Bobbi Jo's cheeks had gone a shade of pink they hadn't been before.

"Why are you blushing?" I asked.

Shaking her head, she once again turned her attention to her twin sister. "Get off him, Betty Sue. Your date is waiting for you. I thought you two were going to Dallas for the night."

"We are," Betty Sue told her. "He wanted to stop off for a drink first."

"Are you drinking too?" Bobbi Jo asked her sister.

"Yes." Betty Sue finally got off me and went to take the man she'd come in with by the hand. "Lance, what would you like to drink. It's on the house, so order whatever you want."

Bobbi Jo wasn't happy with her sister drinking. "I'll serve him liquor but not you. I'm not letting you drink then drive, Betty Sue. You should know that by now."

The girl's hand went to her slender hip. "And just tell me why not?"

"You've got two DWI's under your belt, and you're only twenty-two." Bobbi Jo put a bottle of water on the bar for her sister. "Here you go. And what will you be having, Lance?"

"Jack on the rocks." He walked up to me, extending his hand. "Lance."

I shook his hand. "Cash. Nice to meet you."

"Same." He took the empty seat next to me. "New in town?"

"I am." I took a sip of the now-warm coffee and made a face at the bitterness.

Bobbi Jo didn't waste a second as she not only poured some more into the cup but tossed in a couple of sugar cubes too. "That ought to fix it up for you, Cash."

I couldn't help but smile at her. "Thoughtful of you. Thanks."

Betty Sue sighed. "Well, Lance, hurry up with your drink. I want to get on the road to Dallas so I can drink too."

Bobbi Jo narrowed her eyes at her twin. "That sounds to me like you plan on grabbing some beer and drinking on the road."

"You can't control me." Betty Sue narrowed her eyes right back at her sister. "I *am* a grown woman."

"Yeah, a grown woman who's spent a week in jail each time you got caught drinking and driving. When will you learn?" Bobbi Jo asked her.

"When will you learn to butt out of people's business?" She looked at the coffee I was drinking. "Did he even order that? Or was he having a little too much fun and you forced him to drink that nasty-ass coffee?"

I held up one finger to stop them. "I can fix this if you want me to, Bobbi Jo."

"This isn't your problem, Cash. Thank you, though." Bobbi Jo turned her attention to her sister once more. "Are you forgetting that it was me who not only had to put up the money to bail your ass out of jail, but I also kept it from Dad as long as I could to help you out? Driving to Dallas to get you out wasn't exactly a thing I had time for, either time you wound up in jail there. And by the looks of things, you're headed to a Dallas jail again tonight. Well, I'm not coming to get you if you end up in jail again; I promise you that."

I felt the need to interject once more. "I can help you out, Bobbi Jo. I really can."

Betty Sue looked at me with a sexy smile. "Tell me how you can help out, Cash."

"Only if your sister wants me to," I told her.

Bobbi Jo huffed as she looked at her sister, then me. "How can you help out, Cash?"

Sitting up a little straighter, I offered my services. "I have a limo and driver at my disposal. I also have a private jet too. I could have the driver come pick them up, take them to the airport here then my pilot would take them to Dallas where they could take a cab to wherever they're going."

"Yes!" Betty Sue said as she jumped up and down, clapping. "Now give me a drink, Bobbi Jo. Cash is taking care of it all." Her blue eyes met mine. "Care to join us, Cash?"

I shook my head. "Nope. I'm gonna hang out here."

Betty Sue shook her head as she looked at her sister. "You're off tomorrow. You hired that new guy. You could come too, Bobbi Jo. I bet if you come, then Cash will too."

She was right. But I didn't really want to go. I wanted to hang out with Bobbi Jo alone. So I gave Bobbi Jo a look that I hoped would telegraph my thoughts to her without me having to say anything.

"I've got plans for tomorrow, Betty Sue. If you want to take Cash up on his offer, I suggest you do so. But leave me out of your plans." She filled a glass with coke and rum then put it in front of her sister. "And so help me, Betty Sue, if you call me telling me that you're in jail, I will wring your neck." Then she smiled at me, and that smile was worth everything. "Thanks, Cash."

"Not a problem at all." I sat back in the tall chair, happy I could help ease the girl's mind. It seemed like a lot of weight was on her shoulders where her sister was concerned.

I pulled out my cell and sent a message to Buddy, asking him about giving a ride to some of my friends. He answered immediately that he'd be right down to the bar to pick them up.

I'd never had the resources to do anything that nice before. Looking up, I silently thanked my grandfather for everything. Without what he'd left us, we'd still be struggling every day just to make a buck.

A short time later, Betty Sue and Lance left. With it being Saturday night, the partygoers stayed until the bar closed. I hadn't had anything else to drink and helped Bobbi Jo clean up and lock up so Joey could go home.

"You don't have to stay, Cash," she told me as she put chairs on top of tables so she could mop.

I'd done my fair share of cleaning in my time. "I'll go make the mop water while you sweep the floor. I don't mind helping you, Bobbi

Jo. I even like it. I used to get paid to do things like this. Doing it for fun is kind of cool."

"Fun?" She laughed. "There's nothing fun about cleaning."

All I could do was shrug as I went to make the mop water. To me, it was fun just hanging around with the girl. She was so unlike any of the other girls I'd ever met. She didn't try to act like something she wasn't. She didn't try to flirt with me. She didn't try to make herself as pretty as she could be at every moment just to attract me.

When I came back out with the bucket and the mop, I saw she'd nearly finished sweeping the floor and went to the back to start mopping. "I'm pretty fast at this. Maybe after we're done cleaning, I could give you a lift home."

"I drove my car here." She went to the back to put the broom away.

Hurrying to finish mopping, I tried to think of another way I'd get to spend some more time with her. When she came back out and went to the register to get the money out of it, I came up with another idea. "How about I follow you to your place; you can pack a bag real quick, then I'll take you out to my place? There are tons of empty guest rooms. And you did say you'd come out tomorrow anyway. Why not join me for breakfast. Chef Todd makes some great breakfasts. Ella—that's the maid who my brother Tyrell is sweet on but won't admit it—she said Todd makes Sunday brunches that are to die for. Her actual words, not mine. I rarely say 'to die for.'"

As she put the money into a bank bag, she smiled, and I thought for a moment that she would accept my generous offer. "That's very nice of you, Cash. I like to sleep in on Sundays. That means until two or three in the afternoon. So, you see, I would sleep right through that brunch you're talking about. I meant that I'd come over for dinner tomorrow evening if that's still okay with you."

"Sure." I couldn't hide the disappointment in my voice. "I get it. You work all week, staying up late each night. You need to catch up on your rest sometime. I was just—"

She said, "Thinking you wanted to spend more time together."

Nodding, I smiled at her. "Yeah. Dumb, huh?"

"Wanting to spend more time with me is dumb?" she asked with wide eyes. "I don't think that. I think it's sweet. And I think it sounds like something people who are looking for a relationship do. I want to be perfectly clear with you, Cash. I enjoy your company. I like you. But I like my freedom too."

"Me too." I did like my freedom. "And you're right. I'm asking too much. I'll chill. Maybe it's being in a new town and not knowing many people yet that has me all clinging to you. You're my first friend here, Bobbi Jo."

I liked the way a slow smile traveled over her lips. "That's cool. I think you and I will be great friends, Cash."

I'd had it with just being friends. I wanted something a little more too. Not a lot more, just a little. So I pushed the mop across the floor as I made my way to her.

She watched me as I came closer and closer to her. Moving behind the bar, I mopped all the way up to her feet. "Just because we're friends doesn't mean we can't have a little fun. You know what I'm saying?" I laid the mop handle against the bar next to her then put my hands on her narrow shoulders.

She licked her lips. "I think I understand what you're saying."

"Good." Moving my arms around her, I pulled her close as we looked into each other's eyes. Slowly, I moved in until our lips met, and the way lightning zipped through me told me we had what it took to get a hell of a lot more physical with our friendship.

CHAPTER EIGHT

Bobbi Jo

Fireworks went off inside my head. That had never happened before, and I had no idea what that even meant. All I knew was that my arms were wrapping around him and my lips parted to let him in.

He lifted me up easily, sitting me on top of the bar. I felt his cock throbbing against my already hot pussy. One of his hands moved to cup one of my tits, and my nipples went hard. I moaned with how amazing it felt to be with him that way.

When he moved his mouth off mine, to trail his hot lips up my neck, I could barely breathe. "You kiss better than most, Bobbi Jo."

"You too." I ran my fingers along his arms. "Maybe it's because your muscles are so damn sexy."

He took my hands and then had me untuck his shirt, then he moved my hands underneath it, pressing them to his muscular abs then pecs. "How do you like these?"

"I like them a lot." He let my hands go, and I moved them all over his tight stomach and chest. "Hills and valleys everywhere."

Reaching behind me, he untied my apron then pulled it off me.

His hands moved underneath the back of my shirt, then my bra was unhooked before I knew what was happening.

His hands came around, cupping my tits. "Soft," he whispered.

Even though I hadn't had a thing to drink, I felt drunk. Moving my hands over his, I urged him to caress my tits as I looked into his baby blue eyes. "It's nice being your friend, Cash."

"I like being yours too," he said, then kissed me again. The pure passion that filled me wasn't something I'd ever fully experienced before.

I supposed it was because Cash was the best-looking guy I'd ever kissed. When you added in how well he was built and how much attention he'd paid me in only a couple of days, it all made perfect sense.

He moved one hand down to rub it over my crotch. The heat from it had him groaning, and I knew why. As he pulled his mouth off mine again, I whispered, "It's been awhile. Seems my nether regions are heating up rather rapidly. Please excuse that."

His lips pulled up into a wry grin. "It's been a while for me too. My cock is about to burst through my blue jeans. If you come home with me tonight, I promise to let you sleep as long as you want to. I won't let anyone disturb you, I swear. The beds at my place are kind of amazing. You'll sleep like a baby. Well, afterward, you will."

I acted like I had no idea what he was talking about. "Afterward?"

His eyes danced. "Yeah. After I fuck you like you've never been fucked before."

My breath caught in my throat. No one had ever talked to me that way—raw, purely sexual, and real. Cash left nothing to the imagination. He wanted to fuck me, and I wanted him to.

I suppose the other guys I'd had sex with weren't as passionate, strong, masculine, nor uber-sexy as Cash was. Maybe that was why no one had ever turned me on the way he did. Maybe that was why no one had ever come straight out and told me they wanted to fuck me.

"I don't know about going out to the ranch with you, Cash." I didn't want him to think this was more than what it was—just sex.

"I could go to your place, I guess." He kissed a line along my collarbone.

"No!" I pushed him back as I shook my head. "I live at home. You don't want to meet my parents. Not like that."

He just smiled. "Then come home with me. I'll bring you back to pick up your car whenever you want me to. For now, though, I want you to sit next to me in my truck where I can finger-fuck your hot pussy all the way out to the ranch. I want to feel your hot come all over my fingers."

"Shit," I hissed. No one had ever said anything even remotely like that to me before. "I hope you're as good as your mouth says you are, Cash Gentry."

"I'm better than my mouth says I am, Bobbi Jo Baker." He kissed the soft spot behind my ear. "I asked around about you today and found out a few things—like your last name and the fact that your daddy is the sheriff of this small town. Your mother is a nice lady too. I met her at the feed store this morning."

"How?" I shut up as he sucked a place on my neck that left me speechless.

"You said something to someone about her working there last night. I wanted to meet her. Don't ask me why, because I don't know. But I wanted to see her." His lips brushed across my cheek. "There's something about you, girl. I just want to get all up in you. So, what do you say? Wanna let me?"

My head swirled. My legs shook as he pressed his hard cock against my apex. My hands trembled as I moved them over his shoulders. "When it's over, we'll still just be friends, right? I don't want anything more than that."

"Cool." He kissed my lips softly. "Me neither. Friends with benefits. That's fine with me."

"No sweet names, either. I'm not your baby; you're not my man." I had to make sure we had the rules set. I wasn't going to get involved with anyone. Not yet. I had my life to live first.

I'd seen one friend after another get with a guy, move way too fast, end up in a relationship, which always meant fights. Lots of fights.

Arguing over where to go eat dinner, arguing over why some girl said hi to their man, arguing over why he wore a blue shirt when she told him to wear a green one so it would match with her eyes.

Yeah, I'd had a lot of girlfriends in my lifetime who were extra like that. And I didn't want to become one of them. All of them had said I would be just like them when I found myself a man.

I'd be just at bitchy, overbearing, and insecure as they were. I'd be searching through my man's cell every time I got the chance to make sure he wasn't talking to anyone else. I'd be making him dress in a way that made us look like a couple, so no other woman would dare to even speak to him.

I didn't want to turn into that kind of person. I wouldn't do it. No matter what it took.

So sweet names were out.

He pulled the rubber band out of my hair, releasing my ponytail. "Why would I call you sweet names? That's what couples do. We're not a couple."

My heart pounded as he ran his hands up my arms then put them on either side of my face. "We're friends. And as that, we should help each other out at times. Like I helped you clean up after work, right?"

I nodded, barely coherent. "Yeah."

He took my hand then pressed it to the bulge in his pants. "And now you can help me with this little problem, can't you?"

I nodded again. "Yeah."

He let my hand go so he could place his palm on my hot, jean-covered pussy. "And this seems like it's in need of help too. What kind of a friend would I be if I didn't help you out with this?"

"A bad one." I took a deep breath as I looked at his gorgeous face. "So, we can just help each other out then. No need to think it's anything more than a couple of friends helping each other out. Right?"

"Right." He kissed me again, making me even hotter. His hands moved all over my body and mine did the same to his.

I couldn't remember ever wanting anyone so damn much. Every atom in my body wanted this man. Just as that thought came into my mind, he pressed his cock against my aching pussy and pumped a little.

I gasped as our lips parted. "Cash!"

His fingers pulled at the button on my jeans. "Yeah?"

"You'll have to use a condom." I didn't like taking birth control. I didn't have sex enough to warrant doing that.

"I saw a machine in the men's room. I'll be right back." He stepped back, and I could see the size of the hard-on inside his jeans. "I'll get plenty of them. Don't you worry at all."

Sitting on the bar, I nodded as he took off to the bathroom. My breathing was already erratic. My nipples were hard as rocks when I ran my hands over them. That man was about to rock my world, of that I had no doubt.

But would I be able to rock his?

I'd had sex with four guys. I could count on two hands the amount of times I'd even had sex. The sudden onslaught of nerves had me getting off the bar. Pacing, I thought about how stupid I was for thinking I could do this with a man like Cash.

The sound of the bathroom door creaking open had me looking up, and I must've looked a little crazy. "What's wrong? You're not having second thoughts, are you?"

"I'm not sure."

He raced to me, picking me back up and putting me on the bar again. "Don't have second thoughts, Bobbi Jo."

"You're, well, you're better at this than I am." I bit my lower lip as insecurity filled me. "I've had sex less than ten times, Cash. I'm not great at it."

"So." He took me by the chin. "It's up to me to be great. All you've got to do is let me show you what I can do for you. I'm not looking for anything more than that. I'll take on all the work. You just lay back and relax."

He had no idea how sexually useless I was. "I've never given a blow job."

"So." He smiled at me.

"Not a hand job either."

Still, he smiled. "So."

I had one more thing to admit to him that I was truly afraid would have him changing his mind. "I've never had a sexually induced orgasm either. Not one of the four guys I've had sex with has ever been able to make me come."

"I will definitely make you come, Bobbi Jo. That's a promise." He placed his hand on my crotch. "Want me to prove that to you before I take you home and fuck you senseless?"

"How?" My head swooned as the possibilities rose in it.

He slowly unbuttoned my jeans, then unzipped them. Picking me up a bit, he slid my pants and panties down. Then he sat my bare ass back down on the top of the bar.

All I could do was stare at him as he pushed me to lie back. "Feel free to scream when I make you come, Bobbi Jo. Hearing a woman scream my name while in the throes of ecstasy really does it for me."

"K." I fisted my hands as he kissed my intimate lips, then ran his tongue through my folds, before pushing it into me. Gasping, I already felt a twinge of something I'd never felt before. And within a couple of minutes, I was exploding, crashing, and imploding all at once with his name on my lips. "Cash! Cash! Cash!"

CHAPTER NINE

Cash

A few days after having sex with Bobbi Jo, all I wanted was to have more of the same. Only she wasn't into coming home with me every night. I got Saturday night and Sunday night too, but after that, I was out of luck.

Hump day was upon us, and I had high hopes of using that fact to get back into her pants. I sat at the bar, nursing a beer as Bobbi Jo put away clean mugs into the freezer. "So, happy hump day, Bobbi Jo." I held up my mug to her.

Laughing, she closed the freezer door then turned to look at me. "Happy hump day to you too, Cash."

"So, on that note."

She shook her head. "Nope."

I had no idea why she didn't want to have sex again. With people in the bar, I didn't want to talk too loudly about it, but I had to say something. "You need my help back there this evening, Bobbi Jo?"

She pointed at Joey. "I've got him to help me. Thanks though."

I decided I wouldn't give up. When Joey came back up to the bar to make some more drinks, I said, "How'd you like to go home early tonight, Joey? I can stay and help the boss clean up after closing time."

"Cool," he said as he jerked his head toward a girl sitting at the far end of the bar. "It's my girl's birthday. I planned on taking her to Whataburger after closing anyway."

Bobbi Jo frowned at him. "Well, why didn't you tell me that, Joey? Hell, take off now. There's no reason for your girlfriend to spend her birthday sitting here at this bar, doing nothing." She went to the register and opened it up, pulling out some money. "Here, take this and take her somewhere better than Whataburger." She pulled a bottle of Texas Crown Royal off the shelf and handed it to him. "Take this too. Have a great night and take tomorrow off too."

"Wow," he said as he looked surprised. "Thanks, boss." He held up the bottle and wad of money in his fist too as he shouted to his girl, "Come on, baby, we're going out!"

The smile that lit her up made me and Bobbi Jo smile too as she ran to him and jumped into his arms. "Oh, Joey!"

As the two left, Bobbi Jo and I looked at each other, then I said, "So, can I help you clean up now?"

She nodded. "Yes. But that's all we're going to do."

"Why?" I put the bottle to my lips as I waited for her answer.

She cleaned off the bar. "I don't want you to get used to doing that."

When she got close enough to me that I could whisper, I asked, "Don't you mean you don't want to get to used to doing that? Screaming my name while you break down into a puddle of pleasure must be terrible for you."

Her cheeks went bright red as she turned to walk away from me. She went straight back to the freezer, opened the door then just stood there. "You're bad."

"You're hot." I took another drink as my cock pulsed.

She closed the freezer door then purposely went to work, arranging the bottles on the shelf, so she didn't have to look at me. "You could stop trying to make me that way."

"What's the fun in that?"

Someone yelled about needing more beer, and she had to come back to face me to get some out of the cooler. "Cash, we're not supposed to be trying to turn each other on all the time."

Nodding, I knew we weren't. But she turned me on all the time anyway. "You could stop being so damn cute," I said.

"I literally got out of bed, took a shower, dressed, then came to work," she said. "My hair is in a damp ponytail, I have on no makeup at all, and I forgot to put on deodorant. Still, think I'm so damn cute?"

I wished I didn't, but that did nothing but make her more appealing to me. "Damn, Bobbi Jo, how do you do it?" I had to move a bit to rearrange myself on the barstool. "You're making me uncomfortable here."

"I didn't mean to." She put the four beers on the bar. "Wanna take those to the guys over there?"

"Um, no." I looked her in the eyes. "You gave me a chubby."

She looked perplexed. "How?"

Shrugging, I didn't know exactly how she'd done it. She wasn't even trying. "All I know is that you could fix it if you'd meet me in the back for a few minutes."

"Forget that." She took the beers off the bar then went to serve them.

I watched her in the mirror; her backside swaying with every step. "Here ya go, boys."

As she walked back toward the bar, she caught my eyes in the mirror and smiled. All I knew was that I would be helping her clean up after closing and we'd be alone. And I wouldn't waste a second getting her on her back.

My cock ached for her. I'd never had such sweet pussy in my life —and I'd had plenty to compare it to. Bobbi Jo did things for me that made no damn sense. She didn't even try to turn me on, yet she still did.

Waking up with her in my arms was a pleasant surprise the two mornings I got to spend with her. I was usually the guy who left way before having to wake up with a girl. But waking up with Bobbi Jo was cool.

We'd brushed our teeth together each morning. And she had pulled the sheet off the bed to cover herself each morning too. I had to yank it off her, toss her over my shoulder, and make her get into the shower with me. We laughed a lot. We kissed a lot. And we connected on a level I didn't know I could with a girl.

The door opened, and group of women came in. They were rowdier than anyone else in the bar and Bobbi Jo clued me in as she hurried to fill up frosted mugs with beer. "Wednesday evening church is out. Have you lost your little problem, Cash? Can you help me out now?"

"I wouldn't call it little." I got up as I had gotten rid of the erection. "What would you like me to do?"

"Grab a tray and take these beers to the ladies over there. Watch out; they can get a little handsy." She winked at me. "But they tip good, so forgive them for their trespasses."

"Sweet." I picked up the tray heavy with mugs of beer then headed to their table. "Evening, ladies. How about some cold suds to make your hump day a little better?"

"Halleluiah!" one of the shouted.

Another added, "Praise, Jesus!"

A third quickly picked up her mug of beer, holding it up high. "Nectar of the gods!"

I thought it a bit funny that these church-going ladies loved their beer so much. "So, what church do you ladies go to?"

"Cowboy Church," one of them told me. "That's why we like our beer so much."

Another pinched me on the ass. "You should come on Sunday and check it out. On Sundays, the men barbeque and we all get drunk after the morning service."

"Okay, thanks for the invitation." I moved one woman's hand off my butt as I tried to walk away.

But another one of them grabbed my hand. "So are you single?"

Another hollered, "What's your name?"

Before I could answer, another shouted, "Do you believe in love at first sight?"

I decided to answer the questions in order, "I am single. My name is Cash Gentry. And I do believe in love at first sight."

"Gentry?" one of them asked. "Like Whisper Ranch, Gentry?"

"Yep." I headed back to the bar, but another one of them caught me by the leg, a bit close to the family jewels.

I looked at her hand as she asked, "Can we have services out there sometime?"

Moving her hand, I shrugged. "I'd have to ask my brothers what they think about that first."

"Are they as gorgeous and single as you are, Cash?" A large, dark-haired lady asked.

"Um, kind of." I made sure to get away this time. "I'll be back with more beer in a bit. And maybe a tray of food too." They seemed like they needed something to eat to make sure the alcohol didn't hit them too hard. The spirit of something had already hit them hard enough.

When I caught the smirk on Bobbi Jo's face, I moved in close next to her. "Very funny."

"I know, right?" She laughed. "I see big bucks in your night, Cash."

All I saw was the end of the night. "I see you waking up in my bed in the morning, Bobbi Jo."

Her cheeks went pink. "Don't get ahead of yourself, lover boy."

"I thought you said we couldn't call each other sweet names." I wasn't going to let her off the hook. "If you get to call me lover boy, I'm going to call you something too. Maybe sexy momma."

"I ain't your momma though." She inched away from me.

I grabbed her by the waist. The bar was tall enough that no one could see what I was doing. "No, but you're my little love slave, aren't you?"

"Nope." She pulled away from me, smiling all the while. "I'm not a slave to anyone or thing."

"Bet you are." She couldn't fool me. I knew she liked—no loved—

what I could do for her and to her body. "I'm going to make you beg for it later on tonight, girl. Just wait and see."

A shiver ran through her body, and I watched it tremble. "Hush."

Maybe I was getting too loud. So I got closer. "I think I'll call you cake."

She looked at me with confusion riddling her pretty face. "Cake? And why is that?"

"Because, you are moist, sweet, and I love to eat you." I tickled her tummy, making her squirm.

"Cash!" She stepped away from me as she tried not to laugh. "You're being terrible tonight."

"I'm horny." I didn't see any reason to lie to her.

Putting her hand on her hip, she jerked her head to the table full of women I'd waited on. "Any one of them would be happy to take care of that for you."

"Yeah, I know." I ran my eyes up and down her little body. "But I only want you."

With raised brows, she said, "We're still just friends, you know. If you want one of them, I won't get mad at you. You're a free man—remember that."

"And you're a free woman." I grinned at her. Something about being free to be with anyone I wanted made wanting her that much more appealing. "There's a bar full of eligible men out there. Pick one."

She wagged her finger at me. "First of all, I'm not the horny one here, you are. Second of all, I don't mess with men from the bar. It's bad for business."

"How do you explain me?" I asked.

"I can't." She picked up a bar towel and tossed it to me. "Can you clean up that table the group of guys just left for me?"

Nodding, I said, "Sure. If you can tell me that you'll be waking up in my bed in the morning."

The way her lips quirked to one side made my cock twitch. "You drive a hard bargain."

"I know. I drive other things hard too." Winking, I walked past her, patting her ass as I went by. "My bed, in the morning, waking up in my arms."

"Maybe."

I shook my head. "For sure. You'll see. You'll be begging me later."

She wasn't giving up. "I highly doubt that."

I highly don't doubt it.

CHAPTER TEN

Bobbi Jo

With my body pressed against the wall, his mouth on my cunt, and my hands fisted in his thick hair, I moaned as he pulled his mouth away from me again. "No, Cash. Don't stop. I was almost there."

"Oh, were you? I didn't know," he said as he kissed a trail inside my thigh.

The smell of bleach water from the mop bucket made my nostrils burn. "I think it's time to go. We've been closed for over an hour. People are going to start thinking we're doing more than cleaning in here."

"So." Cash didn't seem to care what people thought. He moved up my body, then pressed his lips to mine before pulling back. "So, are you ready?"

I'd never planned on going home with him. "Can't you just do me here? Then we can go our separate ways, and no one has to know what we're doing."

"Again, Bobbi Jo, I don't care who knows what we're doing. I don't know why you care either. And if you want more, then you know where you can get that." He nibbled on my ear as he ground his hard cock against my throbbing, bare pussy. He'd taken my jeans off long ago, teasing me relentlessly with oral sex, but leaving me just short of an orgasm.

Taking his face in my hands, I said, "I thought you didn't want a girlfriend."

"I don't." He grinned at me. "And I know you don't want a boyfriend. I'm cool with how things are with us. We have great sex. We get along great too. I see no reason to think beyond that point."

"So, what's this thing with wanting me in your bed all the time and waking up in your arms?" That sounded a lot like a relationship to me.

"I like it." He moved his hands down my waist. "You do too. Your wet pussy each morning tells me that, even if you won't."

My body did love his. "But sleeping together seems too intimate to me. Aren't you afraid of what might happen?"

"Like if we'll fall in love?" he asked, then laughed.

The fact he laughed sort of pissed me off. "Is it that funny to you? You think I'm not a person you could fall in love with?"

"First, I don't fall in love. Second, if I did, you could be a person I would do that with. But for now, I like spending time with you in many ways. I like hanging out at the bar with you. I like talking to you. And I really, really like it when my cock is buried deep in that hot pussy of yours."

"Graphic," I mumbled.

"I like to keep it real." He let me go to pull my jeans up that had been around my ankles. "So, let's get going, cake."

"Don't call me that." I zipped up my jeans, then buttoned them. "I'll drive my car over. I want to leave early so I can get back home and sleep until noon."

Taking my hand, he pulled me back to him, holding me tight. "You'll ride with me, and we will sleep together until noon."

"What's the deal with you, Cash? You want to be around me all the time." I'd never had anyone want to be around me so much.

"So?" He played with my hair after pulling it out of the ponytail. "Are you going to say you don't like being around me?"

"I wouldn't know. Since you came to town, I'm rarely *not* around you." I smiled at him. "But that's because you've made it your goal in life to be where I am most of the time."

"And you want me to stop coming around?" he asked but didn't let me go.

"I didn't say that. I just pointed out that it's you coming around me, and not the other way around."

He gripped me tighter, his voice rough and raspy. "Funny, when we're having sex, it's you coming around me."

"It's always sex with you." I took a deep breath to steady myself as he made me feel weird. Like I wanted to take off all my clothes and just get tangled up with him.

Moving me backward, he danced me to the backdoor. Our cars were parked in back. "Probably because sex with you consumes my thoughts. I just want more and more."

I'd never been a sex object to anyone before. It was kind of mind-blowing that someone like Cash thought of me as one. "Is that all I am to you, Cash?"

"Nope." He opened the door behind my back, then danced me out of it. Letting me go, he pulled the door closed then waited for me to lock it.

After locking the door, I looked at my car, but he grabbed my hand and pulled me to his truck. "I really should take my car, Cash."

"Nope." When he made up his mind, there was no changing it. "You haven't begged enough to suit me yet. I've gotta torment you all the way home. I can't do that if you're not sitting next to me in the truck."

"You're still set on making me beg, huh?" I had to laugh.

He opened the truck door then picked me up and sat me in the driver's seat. "Scoot over, cake."

Moving over, I shook my head. "I hate that nickname, Cash."

"Then make up a new one." He slid in behind the steering wheel. "To be honest, I've had to stop myself from calling you baby."

Shaking my head, I wasn't going to get that started. "No way, Cash.

You and I both agreed that we don't want a relationship. I don't want to be your baby."

"But I can be your lover boy?" He started the truck and it roared to life.

"You're not my lover boy," I corrected him. "You are *a* lover boy."

"Okay, so to me you're not my baby, but you *are* a babe." He ran his arm around my shoulders, pulling me tight against his side. "So when I call you baby, I mean that you're a babe. How's that?"

"Not going to fly." I knew using pet names was a bad idea all the way around. "Let's drop the names, other than our real names. It's going to get too complicated if we don't."

"Seems to me that you're afraid you'll fall for me rather easily. I can see that. I mean, I do make you scream my name. And your body melts into mine easily." He moved his hand down in between my legs. "Your pussy is always wet for me."

"In my defense, you have no idea if I get wet for other guys just as easily, Cash." I didn't, but he didn't know that.

"If you did, then you wouldn't have been free tonight." He undid my pants with one hand, then slid that hand into my panties, his fingers sinking into me.

"Oh," I sighed as I gripped his bicep. "Cash. Damn."

Pumping them slowly, he spoke softly, his voice so deep and husky. "You like me inside of you, baby. You want me inside of you. You ache for me just as much as I ache for you. Baby. Baby. Baby."

"Cash," I moaned as he moved his fingers in a way that seemed unreal. "How do you know right where to touch me? How have you found places no other man ever has?"

"Maybe because your body was meant to be pleased by me and me alone." He pumped his fingers a little harder. "Just because we're not in love doesn't mean we weren't meant to please each other."

I didn't want to fall in love. I didn't want all that came with that. But I did want that man to take my body and make it do things only he could make it do. "Please, Cash. Please let me come this time." I didn't want him to stop again. I wanted to feel that rush as my body went over the edge.

Cash could do to me what even a vibrator couldn't do. And I'd tried hard to make it do what he could. I'd been just as horny as he was. At home, I had tried to masturbate, tried to make myself come as hard as he'd made me come. Nothing worked the way he did.

Easing his fingers back and forth, he whispered, "Why should I let you come?"

I couldn't help it as my mouth betrayed me. "Because nothing makes me come like you do."

He chuckled sexily. "See, that wasn't so hard to admit, was it? I'll admit something to you too. I've tried jerking off since I've been fucking you and it doesn't work. I need your tight cunt to get me off. I've never needed anyone to get me off until you came along."

I had no idea what that meant. All I knew was I needed him inside of me—and I needed him now. "Pull over." I pulled his shirt; buttons flew all over the cab of the truck as they ripped off from the pressure.

He pulled over, parking the truck then pushing me to lie back on the seat. "You want it now?"

Nodding, I wanted it right then and there. "Please, Cash. Please fuck me like only you can."

He shimmied my jeans the rest of the way off, then pulled a condom out of his pocket before pushing his jeans down just enough to release his massive cock. He held the condom out to me. "You put it on for me, baby." His smile told me that he wasn't going to stop calling me that.

So I decided to mess with his head too. "K, honey bunch."

As I rolled the condom down his long shaft, my heart pounded. He whispered in my ear. "Tonight, I'm going to teach you how to suck me off. That way, when I get too riled up for you, you can take care of me with just your mouth."

I couldn't explain why my mouth began to water with what he'd said. "You want me to learn how to give you head so I can do it almost anywhere?"

"Yep." He lifted my face, holding my chin. "In the bathroom at the bar. In the back room of the bar. In the cab of my truck. Anywhere at all."

"And how will you fix me up?" I wasn't going to be the one doing all the fixing in this thing.

"Are you kidding?" He laughed. "Haven't I shown you that?"

"So, you'd just take me into the back of the bar, drop my jeans, and eat me out?" I felt hot and shocked. "While people are there? Like right in the next room?"

He nodded. "Yep."

No one had ever made me so hot in my life. I gazed into his eyes as he spread my legs apart, then moved in between them, thrusting hard into me. We both grunted with the force. "I suppose we'll have to learn to be quiet if you want to do this in close proximity to others."

"Well, we're alone right now, so feel free to make all the noise you want." He moved harder, knocking the air out of my lungs. "I love it when you say my name."

"Cash," I whispered as I looked into his blue eyes. What I felt scared me a little. I could so easily fall into the man and never come up for air again.

CHAPTER ELEVEN

Cash

Bobbi Jo had made some hot nights for me, and I wasn't thinking about anyone else as I walked down the street toward the Dairy King to grab one of their juicy cheeseburgers. Whistling as I walked, I felt a hand run across my back as a saucy female voice whispered, "Miss me, cowboy?"

Spinning around, I found Bobbi Jo wrapped in my arms, her lips pursed for a kiss. Who was I not to oblige the young lady? Leaning in, our lips met, hers parted, and our tongues entwined.

Her breasts felt the tiniest bit smaller as they squished against my chest. Her kiss tasted like cinnamon instead of the usual spearmint. And the way she moved her tongue didn't seem right.

Pulling back, I looked into her eyes. The devilish sparkle told me all I needed to know. "Betty Sue, you little hussy, you." I let her go quickly, then ran my hand over my mouth as if wiping away the kiss.

Her fingers moved over her lips. "What a kisser you are, Cash Gentry." She gave me a sly wink. "No wonder my sister has been keeping late hours since you moved into town. You know, she and I share lots of things. You could be one of them."

I didn't want to be rude, but I wasn't into what she thought I was. "Well, *I'm* not something you two will be sharing."

"Oh?" She looked inquisitive. "You planning on getting serious with my sister?"

I shook my head; seriousness wasn't my intention at all. "Not too serious. But serious enough that I ain't about to start swapping spit on the regular with her twin sister. You shouldn't even play games like that, Betty Sue. Don't you think it might bother your sister at least a little to know that we kissed?"

"I don't see why it would bother her." She licked her lips as if tasting me on them and liking what she'd found. "She and I have been with the same guys, Cash. This town is small. There's only so many girls to go around. The fact is, most of us girls have dated the same guys at one time or another." She looped her arm through mine. "Where are you headed?"

"To get a burger." I started walking that way again. "You're more than welcome to join me." I thought I should lay out some ground rules though. "As long as you understand that I don't wish to date you or do anything else like that with you."

"I see." She pulled the band out of her long blonde hair to shake it out. The sweet scent of honeysuckle eased past my nose. "Well, you can't blame me for trying now, can you?"

I could and would blame her for trying. If any of my brothers had done something that two-timing, I would've whooped their asses right quick and in a hurry. But I really had no idea what the relationship between the two sisters was, so I wasn't about to go making too much of a stink about what she'd pulled. "Just chill, girl. That's all I'm saying."

"I only wanted to convey my thanks for letting me borrow your jet, and the limo rides too." She gave my arm a little squeeze. "I've never even been on a plane before. It was awesome."

"How'd Lance like it?"

"Who?" She smiled at me, knowing exactly who I was talking about.

I opened the door for her as we got to the little café.

"Oh, thank you, Cash. You are such a gentleman." She moved through the door before me then waited for me to be at her side where she once again looped her arm through mine.

I could tell she didn't want to mention Lance. Although I had no idea why that was, I felt it best not to dig too much into her love life. "So, I hear the cheeseburgers here are great. You want one?"

She ran her free hand over her small waist. "Not me. I only eat salads."

Betty Sue wasn't one ounce heavier than her sister who ate whatever she wanted. "You got some weight problem that your twin doesn't?"

"What?" She looked confused and a little horrified.

"Bobbi Jo eats whatever she wants to and it doesn't affect her weight at all. So why do you only eat salads?" I thought about it a second as we took seats across from each other at a booth. "Oh, wait. I know why that is. Hey, look, you eat what you want to. I'm not a romantic prospect anyway. You can think of me like a brother. Brothers don't give a damn what their sisters eat."

"How would you know, Cash?" she asked with a grin. "You only have brothers."

"Well, it's the same with them. We don't care what anyone eats, really. And here's a hint for you. Men do not care if you eat like a rabbit or not. It doesn't make them think any less or more of you. As a matter of fact, if it makes us feel anything, it's sorry for you." I smiled at the waitress who came to us. "Hey, darling. We'll have two of those cheeseburger meals you got up there on the menu. I'll have onion rings and a coke with mine." I nodded at Betty Sue. "And you?"

"A chocolate milkshake and some fries with mine. And no onions or pickles on my burger." She put her hand over her mouth. "They give people bad breath."

"You might as well have them," I said. "You ain't kissing no one anyhow."

She kicked me under the table. "You hush. You don't know what I've got planned for after lunch."

Shrugging, I said, "You're right. Seeing how you like to accost men from behind and smooch away right there on the sidewalk and all."

I got another kick for saying that and a shocked expression from the waitress. Betty Sue growled, "Just leave them off, please." She glared at me. "And you need to learn to watch what you say."

Nodding, I could tell from both their reactions that I did need to learn to do that. "Gotchya."

After the waitress walked away, Betty Sue changed her tone as she said, "So, anyway, what do you think about living at the ranch? Oh, and when are you gonna get around to inviting me out to see it?"

I'd never had any intentions of inviting her out to see the ranch. "After what you just pulled, I don't think it's a real good idea to invite you out to my home."

Rolling her eyes, she huffed. "I told you: my sister and I have kissed lots of the same guys. You're nothing special, Cash Gentry."

"Whoa!" I thought that was a bit uncalled for. "No reason to hit below the belt. And about that kiss ... you gonna tell Bobbi Jo or should I do it?"

"I don't see that either one of us needs to tell her anything." She pulled a mirror out of her purse and looked at herself in it. "You could've told me that I needed more lip gloss, Cash." She smiled at me sexily. "You've kissed it all off my lips, you bad boy."

"Okay, so I'll tell her then." I wasn't about to not let Bobbi Jo know what her sister had done.

I'd been through this sort of thing before: kissed a girl while messing with another. Not that we were serious either, but when a third party tells the person you are currently messing with that they saw you locking lips with someone else, people tend to get pissed. And I didn't want Bobbi Jo to get mad at me for something I didn't purposely do.

Not that I thought she'd get mad, but I wanted to play it safe. I liked hanging with the girl. And I particularly liked the sex. I wasn't about to let anyone mess that up for me. Bobbi Jo and I had some pretty serious heat, and there were still plenty of things I would've liked to do with her—and to her. Something like this could throw a monkey wrench in what I had planned for that girl.

Putting on a fresh coat of lip gloss, Betty Sue seemed to be contemplating things. Finally, she put her purse and makeup away, then looked at me. "I'll do it. It wasn't your doing anyway."

"Good girl." I smiled at her as the waitress brought our food. "And if she asks me anything about it, I'll tell her the truth. So make sure you do the same."

"I will." She looked at the food in her red basket, and I saw the sparkle in her eyes. "This looks great. Fattening, but great."

"Enjoy," the waitress said before leaving us again.

"If you eat it all, I'll give you a dollar." I laughed as I took a bite of my burger.

"One lousy buck?" she asked with a frown. "So, I'm eating lunch with one of the only three billionaires in Carthage, and all I'm offered is a dollar to eat all the food he's already paying for."

"Yep." I picked up one of her fries. "Except this fry." I popped it into my mouth. "This one was calling my name."

She reached over to steal an onion ring. "So, I'll take this to replace it then."

I smiled as I watched her eat it. "I think that's a fair trade." As long as I had someone from Bobbi Jo's family around, I thought I'd ask some questions of the girl. "So, has Bobbi Jo brought many boys home to meet the family?"

"Nope." She took a little nibble of her burger.

"Take a damn bite, Betty Sue," I urged her. "Enjoy the thing."

She took a bigger bite—nothing huge though. "Yum."

"I know." I took a drink of my coke. "So, why hasn't she ever brought anyone to meet the family? She told me about your mother working at the feed store. And from your mom, I learned your father is the sheriff of Carthage. Is that the reason she's never brought anyone home to meet that family?"

She put her finger on her nose as she chewed her food, then nodded as she swallowed. "Yep. You got it, detective. We don't bring home boys to meet our daddy. He's not real receptive if you know what I mean. Mom's nice. Dad's ..." She hesitated. "Well, he's just Dad. Gruff, doesn't trust many people, and mostly he's always in a bad mood. I suppose dealing with so many bad people have made him that way. I figure he had to have been okay at least when he met our mom. She's not the type to care for grouches. But she's married to one now. That's for sure."

"So, he's grouchy and doesn't trust people." I didn't think that sounded too good. But then again, I wasn't trying to be Bobbi Jo's boyfriend. "Well, that makes sense then."

"You wanted her to bring you home or what?" she asked with a quizzical expression.

"No." I took another bite of my burger. "She just doesn't talk much about her personal life."

"Yeah," Betty Sue agreed. "My sister is more of a listener than a talker. I guess that's why she makes such a great bartender."

"Yeah, guess you're right." As we sat there eating, both of us got quiet.

Finally, she said, "You know, you're not so bad, Cash. I've never kissed a guy and had them not want more."

Raising my brows, I thought that kind of an odd thing to say. "Even someone who was actively hanging with your sister?"

She nodded. "Yep."

With her answer, I had to wonder just what kind of family Bobbi Jo was from. Sisters kissing the same boys ... what else did they do with them?

CHAPTER TWELVE

Bobbi Jo

Cleaning up the bedroom, I looked over at Betty Sue's side of the room we'd shared our whole lives. "Such a pig." I kicked a pair of barely-there underwear of hers that had somehow made it to my side of the floor. "Yuck." They flew to her side of the room, now covered in a pile of dirty clothes, dishes, and bits of paper for some reason.

Hearing the front door to our small, two-bedroom house open, I knew it had to be Betty Sue coming in. "Bobbi Jo? You here?"

My car was in the drive, so she knew I was. "Yep. What tipped you off, Columbo?"

She opened the bedroom door and looked at the heap of crap on her side of the room. "Cleaning, I see. Just once, would it kill you to put my dirty clothes in the washing machine instead of piling them up this way?"

"Have you ever, even once, put my clothes in the wash?" I found one of her many bobby pins on my desk. Picking it up, I tossed it over to her side. "How in the hell do your things end up on my desk? How?" I looked at her for an answer.

All I got was a shrug. "You must use them. That's what I think anyway."

I'd never used a bobby pin in my life. "Sure, Betty Sue."

Moving some things off her bed, covered in stuff, she took a seat. "So, guess who I ate lunch with just a little while ago?"

I had no idea and no care to guess or even to know. "You know I don't care at all, right?"

"You will." She kicked off her shoes then laid back on the filth covering her bed.

"Yuck." I pointed at her and her lack of hygiene. "I can't remember when you last washed your sheets. And you're lying on old food, old clothes, old—God only knows what. Have you no shame?"

She shrugged. "Not really. I think you got all the shame and I was born without any. Thanks a lot for hogging it all, sister." Her lips pulled into a smile. "Guess what I ate today?"

"Don't care." Why she thought I'd care about what she ate, which was most often salads, I had no clue.

"A cheeseburger. And the whole thing too. And I drank all my milkshake and ate all my fries, and I got this dollar for doing it too." She pulled a buck out of her bra. "See." She wiggled it back and forth.

"Whoopee!" I ran my finger in a circle in the air. "Look at you, eating all your junk food. Now, if you'd said you ate a whole plate of green beans, I might be impressed. Chowing down on crap doesn't exactly make me proud of you, Betty Sue."

With a nod, she agreed. "Yeah. I'm not proud I ate all that bad-for-you food either. I did want to order my usual salad, but *he* wouldn't let me."

"He?" I wasn't actually intrigued. I had an idea that she'd gone out to eat lunch with a guy.

"Yes." She smiled as she looked up at the ceiling. "He."

I waited for her to say something else, but she didn't say a word, just stared at the ceiling with that stupid smile on her face. "So, who is he?" I don't even know why I asked. I did not care at all.

"Cash." Her eyes cut to me.

"My Cash?" I felt something cold move through my body, like a river of snakes. My skin began to crawl.

"Yours?" she asked. "I thought you two weren't serious."

"So?" I tried to shake off the terrible feeling I'd gotten. "How did you two end up eating lunch together?"

My sister had always been notorious for not only flirting with the guys I'd been interested in, but she'd done a lot more than that with them too. The way she was smiling filled me with dread.

Have I lost Cash to her too?

"Promise me something first." She sat up, sitting cross-legged on her bed.

"Why?" I wasn't feeling any better about things.

"Because I'm your sister and I'm asking for you to promise me something first. So, please promise me you won't get mad." She looked at me with wide eyes.

Now that I knew I was definitely going to be mad, I crossed my fingers behind my back. "I promise." I didn't say what I promised, just that I did. In my mind, I finished the sentence: *To kick your ass if you did anything more than just eat with Cash.*

"Okay, well, you know how I used to test guys to make sure they really liked you back in high school?" she asked.

Of course I remembered that. Betty Sue would pretend she was me and get the guys who liked me to kiss her. Afterward, she'd admit who she was and that she thought they had a much better connection than what the guy and I had. And the fact that she put-out pretty much made it so that every guy she'd tested went for her, leaving me in the dust.

So, naturally, my blood began to boil. Long gone was the cold river full of snakes that had run through me—now I felt like lava flowed through my veins. But my voice stayed nice and calm as I said, "I remember."

"Yeah, so, anyway, I saw Cash walking down the sidewalk in town." She made a wolf-whistle. "And boy, that cowboy's ass is sure fine."

"I'm aware of that." I bit my tongue so I could wait to hear it all. "And then what happened?"

"Um, well, I really couldn't help myself." She hugged herself. "He's just so hot, you know?"

"Yep." Of course I knew how hot he was. "So what happened?"

All of a sudden, she decided to backtrack. "Okay, anyway, at lunch I was going to order a salad, and he said that I needed to get a burger and that I didn't have a weight problem. And I wasn't sure what that meant. Like, was he looking at my body? I didn't know. And then he went on to say how guys don't actually care if a girl eats salads or not. Like, they just plain don't care what girls eat. You know what I'm saying?"

Of course I knew what she was saying. What I didn't know was what the hell she'd done with my man. "Can you maybe just be specific, Betty Sue?"

"Oh, I can see your eyes are getting a little cloudy." She smiled. "Anyway, so I did get the burger and fries and stuff, and he was all, 'I'll give you a dollar if you eat it all.' Which I was like, 'I don't need your dollar, rich guy.' Or something along that line anyway."

I was starting to lose it. "What happened?" Like I cared about the damn food!

"What happened is that I ate all the food. Like every last bite." She laughed. "Never have I ever eaten that much food. But Cash is so funny and cool that I ate it all without even noticing what I'd done."

"And then?" I clenched my fists as I waited for more. I just knew instinctively that there was more—much more.

"Okay, well then we left, and I came home, and he went—well, he didn't say where he was going." She huffed. "He can be so closed-lipped sometimes. Anyway, what I was asking you to promise me about was what happened before we got to the Dairy King."

I saw her through a shower of sparks as my meltdown was close at hand. "What happened?"

"I don't think you'll care. It's not like it hasn't happened before. And I told him that. I told him we did that sort of thing all the time and it didn't even need to be mentioned." She waved her hand through the air. "But Cash was determined that one of us tell you about it and I said it should be me."

It was imminent; the combustion was going to occur. "What happened?" If I had to ask that again, I would rip her head off.

"So, I saw him and his cute ass," she said, then cocked her head. "He's got a great walk, doesn't he?"

I nodded. "He does."

"Anyway, I saw that ass, that walk, and when I came up behind him, I smelled leather and something smoky, and then I said something cute." She looked up as if trying to remember what she'd said that was so damn cute. "I think I said 'what's up, cowboy?' or something like that."

"That's not so bad." I began to let some of my anger slip back a bit.

"Yeah, it's not, right?" she asked before continuing. "So he turned around. His eyes lit up. He grabbed me, took me into his arms and ..." She stopped talking.

"What?" I was already shaking; I might as well hear the rest by that point. "He did what?"

"Kissed me."

My eyes began blinking really fast. My heart stopped beating. My palms felt like knives where being jabbed into them and that's when I realized my fingernails were dug into them. "Kissed you?"

She nodded. "Yeah. He kissed me."

Time stood still, the room began to swim, and I suddenly was flying. Over the pile of her dirty laundry I went. My fist hit her in the chin first. After that, I felt her silky hair in my hand as I yanked it. I think I was trying to yank it all out—make her bald. "You *slut!*"

"Stop!" she shrieked. "Don't make me hurt you, Bobbi Jo!"

I couldn't feel a thing—except super pissed. "You're dead!"

Slapping began, punches followed. My nails dug into her flesh; hers dug into mine. It was a free-for-all.

"Stop!" my sister screamed.

"I hate you!" I was going to do it this time. I was going to kill her.

I'd come close to doing it before, especially when she'd come to the movie theater where John Parker and I were on a date back in tenth grade. I'd gotten up to go use the bathroom, leaving him alone in the dark. That's when my twin sister went to take my place. She took his hand and stuck it in a place I wouldn't have dared stick it. When I came back, they were making out hardcore. I couldn't believe it.

I left without saying a word, without my popcorn, and without the guy I thought really liked me. And I cried all the way home.

Later, I got a phone call from John, telling me how he had thought it was me the whole time. Well, until they walked out into the light and he remembered that I'd had on a red shirt and jeans. Betty Sue had on a blue tank top and shorts.

I thought his apology meant we were back on. But he wasn't finished talking. He went on to let me know that he liked me and all, but he and my sister had more of a connection than he and I did.

There was no physical fight between my sister and me that day. But I did almost kill her. As silently as she'd slipped into my seat next to John at that theater, I'd silently slipped laxatives into her milk that night at dinner.

When she couldn't get off the toilet that night, not even to answer the phone when John called her to see if she'd like to join him for a movie once again that same day, my parents took her to the emergency room. She was severely dehydrated and to hear her say it, had almost died. And I had to admit what I'd done.

We fell off her bed now as we fought like wolves, gouging, slapping, biting, yanking, and even kicking. This time, I would make sure she knew I was mad as hell at her and not taking any more of her crap.

CHAPTER THIRTEEN

Cash

"Hey, the sign's off, Bobbi Jo." I flipped on the neon open sign on the bar's front window to let everyone know the place was open. "It's dead in here because you forgot to turn this on."

The dim light inside the bar made it difficult to see her clearly, but it looked like she had something held to her face. "Damn. I totally forgot about that. Thanks, Cash."

"It's only fifteen minutes after opening time anyway." I walked over to the bar. The closer I got to her, the more confused I became. "Why are you holding a bag of frozen peas on your eye?"

Pulling the green-and-white bag away from her face, she revealed a swollen, purple-and-black bruised eye. "This is why I've got a bag of frozen peas on my eye, Cash."

Reaching out, I barely touched her swollen lips. "Wanna tell me what the hell happened to you?"

"I got into a fight." She turned away from me as the door opened, letting in a dusty trail of light.

"A fight?"

She nodded then asked the man who'd come in, "What can I get you?" Not that she turned to face him; her back was still to us both.

"Whatever you got on tap," he said as he went to the pool tables in the back.

I walked around to the back of the bar. "I'll take care of him. Have you taken anything for the pain?"

"Pain?" She laughed. "I'm not hurt."

After pulling a frosty mug out of the freezer, I gave Bobbi Jo the once over and what I found told me she was hurting. "So, those bruises on your arms don't hurt at all? And those scratches on your neck don't either?"

"Nope." She leaned over to get something from under the bar and winced.

So now I knew she had some midsection trauma too. "And those ribs of yours are just fine too? No pain there?"

"No pain anywhere. Just some bruises and stuff." She pulled out the cutting board and the knife she used to cut up the various fruits she used for the cocktails.

I took the beer to the guy who'd come in, just as more people began to come into the bar. It was a Friday night; the place would soon be packed. When I came back up to stand at Bobbi Jo's side while she winced with pretty much every move she made, I asked, "Is Joey coming in tonight?"

"He'll be here at eight," she said as she put four bottles of beer on the bar. "I'm okay, Cash. Really. Go sit down. I can handle this. It's not even bad yet."

"You don't look all right. You look like hell, to be honest with you. A little makeup might have been a good idea." I dodged a punch she threw at me.

"Shut up, jack ass." She turned back to look at the door as more people came streaming in. "But I guess I should use your help if you're offering it. Just until Joey comes in."

"You got it, babe." I ignored her frown as I got to work. There was no way I could just sit on my ass and watch her gimping around so slowly and painfully.

Whether she admitted it or not, that girl was feeling some pain. And for some reason, she didn't want me to know who'd done that to her. I couldn't understand why she'd want to keep that a secret. But I left it alone for now. The place was getting busy, and there wasn't time to talk anyway.

After Joey came in, there was still plenty of work to be done, so I kept on helping them. I liked it. It was a nice change of pace from what I'd been doing all day—riding one of the horses around the ranch, checking the fences to make sure that none of them had holes or openings.

It was crazy how many times I had found places where things had gone through and either broken wires or moved them in a way that a calf could easily get out. I'd seen Mr. Castle while I was out that day and had told him to come to the bar have a cold one on me tonight. So when he came in, all duded up in a pearl-snap, black western shirt and matching cowboy hat, I had to whistle at him. "Hey there, sharp-dressed man." I slid a frosty mug full of beer to him as he took a seat at the bar. "Glad you decided to come by."

"Yeah," he said then took a drink, placing the mug back on the bar. "It's been some time since I've gotten out of the house. I thought I could use a night out." He scanned the loud and crowded bar. "And what a night it is."

"Yep, you picked a good one." I jerked my head toward a table. "We've got a full table of women over there just waiting for some smooth cowboy to ask them to dance."

He smiled. "Maybe after a beer or two. It's been a long time since I've cut a rug."

Bobbi Jo came up to my side. "Oh, hi."

I had to laugh as Mr. Castle couldn't stop the stunned expression that came over his face. "What the hell happened to you?" He cleared his throat then held out his hand. "Richard Castle, by the way."

Bobbi Jo shook his hand. "Bobbi Jo Baker. It's a pleasure to meet you, Mr. Castle. You're legendary around this town. It's a wonder we've never met before." She ran her hand in a circle around her battered face. "And this is just something that happens when siblings disagree on things."

So, she'd gotten into a fight with her sister. I had that much now. "How'd Betty Sue turn out?"

"You don't see her around, do ya?" She smiled, then winced as the action must've hurt her busted lip. "Ow. More frozen peas." She nodded at Mr. Castle. "It's really nice to meet one of Cash's neighbors and Joey's uncle. Thanks for coming. And your drinks are on the house tonight, being that this is your first ever visit to The Watering Hole."

"How nice. Thank you," he said. "I promise not to drink your establishment dry."

"I'm sure you won't." She left to take care of other customers as I watched her hobble away.

Seemed she'd hurt her ankle too. It must've been a pretty tough fight for all the injuries she had. I had to wonder, as the night went on, just why the sisters had fought.

One thought kept coming to mind. The kiss Betty Sue had stolen from me. But why would Bobbi Jo get into a physical altercation over something like that?

We weren't exclusive. She wouldn't even let me call her baby in public and barely in bed. So, why would she care so much about the kiss that she'd get into a fight with her twin sister over it?

Or was it something else altogether and I was just being stupid?

Girls could get into fights over stupid things, that much I knew. Maybe it was because Betty Sue had used her razor or borrowed some clothes and ruined them. That sounded much more reasonable than the two of them getting into a tussle over me and that stolen kiss.

As the night went on, then came to a close, the patrons filtering out a little at a time, I finally found the time to put to the screws to her about what had really happened.

In the back, as I was gathering up a few empty boxes to throw the empty aluminum cans in for recycling, I caught her alone for once.

"Hey." I put the boxes down, then went to pin her between me and the wall just as she came out of the walk-in cooler.

"What?" She looked off to one side.

Taking her by her chin, which also had a slight bruise on it, I kissed her swollen and cut lips gently. "Tell me what happened."

"My sister and I got into a fight." She looked me in the eyes.

"*Why* did you get into a fight with her?" I kissed her again, light and easy.

She ran her hands up my arms then around my neck. "It doesn't matter."

"It does to me." Moving in, I trailed a line of kisses up her neck, making sure to peck each scratch.

Her chest rose with a heavy sigh. "I really would rather not talk about it, if that's okay with you."

"It's not okay with me. I want to know what had you two fighting like you were in a cage match." It seemed neither of them had even tried to get away.

With a nod, she knew I was on to something. "It was in our little bedroom. There wasn't much room to get away from each other. I think that's why it went on as long as it did."

Kissing the soft spot behind her ear, I whispered, "And why did it start?"

She moaned as I used the tip of my tongue to entice her. "Oh, Cash, what you do to me should be illegal."

"Yep." I didn't let up on her as I ran my hands up into her hair, releasing the ponytail so I could get that silky stuff between my fingers.

The way her hands moved over my back, her nails gently running over my shirt, made me want her right then and there. "Cash, I think I heard Joey walk out the front door. We should really go make sure that's what I heard."

"That would mean that I would have to let you go. And I don't want to let you go." I kissed a line from her neck to her lips.

Moaning softly, she wrapped her legs around my waist and kissed me back. Then the sound of Joey's voice said, "Guys, I'm leaving now."

Pulling my mouth off hers, I called out, "See you tomorrow, Joey!"

Then the sound of the door closing came, and I knew we were all alone. Her eyes searched mine then she asked, "If our fight was kind of about you, would that make you mad at me?"

"Mad?" I shook my head. "But confused, yes."

"She told me, Cash." She looked a bit on the sad side as her legs dropped, her feet going back to the floor. "You guys kissed."

"Not on purpose. Did she make sure you knew that?" I held her tight as I felt her trying to move out of my arms and I wasn't going to let that happen.

"What do you mean, not on purpose?" The way she looked at me told me Betty Sue hadn't been completely honest with her.

"I thought she was you, Bobbi Jo. As soon as I realized she wasn't you, I stopped the kiss and let her know I wasn't into her that way." I couldn't help but smile as she looked relieved. "But what I don't understand is why you would get into a fight with anyone over me. It's not like we're serious. I don't want you getting yourself hurt over me."

Her jaw went tight as her eyes glazed over. "I know we're not serious, Cash. You don't have to remind me."

"I mean, I'm a free agent," I said, trying to rile her up. "As are you, Bobbi Jo."

Her hands moved, coming up between us then landing on my chest. "Yeah, I know that. Look, can you just back up? I've got things to do."

Oops, riled her up too much, it seems.

CHAPTER FOURTEEN

Bobbi Jo

With Cash all up on me, I couldn't think straight. I'd asked him to back up but he hadn't moved, so I had to add, "Please, Cash. Let me go."

"You're mad." He retained his hold on me.

"No." I pushed him gently but firmly on his chest. "I've just got things to do is all."

His hands loosened on my body, he stepped back, and I moved away from him. Even though I knew we weren't exclusive, I didn't like to think about him being with other girls—especially not my sister.

"The kiss wouldn't have ever happened without her sneaking up on me that way, Bobbi Jo. I want you to know that. Our lack of a serious relationship wasn't why I quit kissing her when I realized it wasn't you. I honestly don't like her in a romantic way at all." He leaned back on the wall, placing one foot on it, looking hot as hell as he just stood there.

"Yet, you invited her to eat lunch with you." I hadn't even allowed myself to think about that fact. Why he'd done that was still a mystery to me.

"She *is* your sister, Bobbi Jo." He looked down as if trying to come up with a plausible excuse for taking her to lunch—a thing he and I hadn't even done.

"Yeah, well what about me?" I went to pick up a case of beer to take to the front to put into the cooler. It was a thing I usually did the following day, but I wanted to stay busy so he couldn't wrap me in his arms and stop me from thinking. "My sister has taken a whirlwind trip on your jet. She's ridden in your limo. And now she's eaten a meal with you as your date. I haven't done any of those things."

"Jealousy," he said as he smiled at me. "You're jealous."

"I'm not jealous. I'm just confused. Are you dating my sister but having sex with me?" I knew better than that but had to say it. "And now you've kissed her too. You've held her in your arms, Cash. What if the same thing had happened between me and one of your brothers?"

"It better not ever happen." He moved across the room quickly, taking the heavy case of beer out of my arms. "Let me do that."

"I can handle it." I tried to reach for it, but he was already too far away. I followed him to the bar, watching him as he put the beer into the cooler. "So, how was that kiss?"

"It wasn't you." He put away the last beer then looked at me. "She's not you."

"And *I'm* what you want?" I asked as my heart pounded.

"Am *I* what *you* want?"

I had no idea why I was the way I was, but commitment was a thing I shied away from. "You're what I want for now."

"Ditto." He strolled over to me, put his fingers on my chin lightly. "You're what I want for now too. You know what else I want?"

I shook my head.

"I want you and I to go do something Sunday and Monday while you're off work. I'm thinking something really cool. We can take the limo and the jet and do anything you want." His hands moved slowly until he was wrapped around me. "Maybe out to Maine to get some fresh-off-the-boat lobster."

"That's a bit much." I did like lobster though.

"I know it is." He kissed me. "But what good am I as a billionaire if I don't take my best girl out once in a while?"

I didn't like being called his best girl. "Nope, you can't call me that either."

He nodded. "Okay then. How about the chick I'm currently screwing?"

"Best girl it is." I smiled, and it hurt my busted lip when I did. "Ow." I put my fingers to it. "This was so stupid."

He pressed his lips to the top of my head as he swayed back and forth with me. "If it helps you at all, I thought about what I would've done if one of my brothers had done the same thing to you that your sister did to me."

"And what did you think about that?" I had a pretty good idea he wouldn't be cool with it at all.

"I thought I would most definitely kick some ass if that ever happened." He chuckled. "But I was pretty sure I would be the only one punching if that happened. Why did Betty Sue fight back instead of running away?"

"I have no idea. She really should've run. She was in the wrong after all." I raised my right hand to look at my red and swollen knuckles. "I gave her two black eyes—way worse than this shiner she gave me. Her nose was bleeding, her mouth was too, and she was wheezing something awful when I finally got off her."

He looked a little shocked. "Wow."

"I know."

"I don't know if I'm going to ever want to get on your bad side." He ran his hand over my cheek. "You're kind of a badass."

"No, I'm not." I wasn't proud of myself for beating my sister up. And I knew once my father found out what I'd done, there would be hell to pay. "My father is going to let me have it when he sees my sister in the morning. This is assault. He won't let me forget that fact."

"He won't put you in jail, will he?" he joked.

But what he didn't know was that my father might very well do something like that to me. "Dad doesn't put up with lawbreakers."

"Then I think I had better keep you with me." He ran his hand down my arm, taking my hand. "If he can't find you, then he can't string you up or lock you up."

"You'd hide me out?" I thought that was sweet of him. "Even though I'm a cold-blooded sister-beater?"

Shrugging, he pulled me to go along with him. "Like I said, if the shoe were on the other foot, I would've clocked a man too. Any man. Not just my brothers. But my brothers would definitely get it worse than some stranger."

I held back, digging my feet in to stop him from taking me any further. "Wait. Are you saying that if I told you that any other man had kissed me, you would beat him up?"

Turning to face me, he ran his hand over my cheek again. "I don't know. I do know I would beat the hell out of my brothers for doing it. You girls share a bedroom, huh?"

I nodded. "Yeah. It's not going to be real comfy in there for a while, I guess."

"I'm serious. I want you to come stay with me. At least until things calm down. It's the least I can do for you. Although I can't say this is my fault, I also shouldn't have been so quick to grab and kiss a woman when the woman in my life has an identical twin in the same town." He turned to head toward the door again with me in tow. "It just wasn't a smart thing for me to do."

"Maybe if I told you more about my sister and her penchant for fucking me over where the male species is concerned, you might've been a bit more careful about kissing a girl who looks like me." I knew I hadn't really let him in on how Betty Sue was. "She has not only right out stolen guys I was interested in, but she's given me a bad rep a few times by claiming to actually be me and doing things I wouldn't have ever done."

"Well, if that's the case, then your father shouldn't be too mad at you for finally whopping her ass." He stopped as we got to the door. "This is the first time you've fought her like this, isn't it?"

"It is." We'd had a few smacks between us but nothing this bad. "It got out of hand really quick. I saw red, then black, then nothing at all. I honestly didn't know I was such a savage." I began to feel a tiny bit bad about what I'd done to my twin. "I even pulled a chunk of her hair out."

"Damn, baby." He opened the door and we went out.

I locked the door, then he picked me up, carrying me to his truck. Wrapping my arms around his neck, I gazed into those baby blue eyes of his. "Baby? What did I tell you about that?"

"Right now, I don't care what you've told me about that." He put me down to open the door of his tall, four-wheel-drive truck, then picked me up, sliding me into the driver's seat. I scooted over as he got inside and took the wheel. "Call me a Neanderthal if you want to, but the fact that you got into a fistfight over me is making me hot as hell for you."

I ran my hand in a circle around my battered and bruised face. "Even with this mug of mine?"

The way he smiled made my heart skip a beat. "Even with that mug of yours." He leaned in to kiss me and my breath froze in my lungs.

I'd never been in love before, so I had no idea what that felt like. But what I felt when he kissed me that time was different. It felt deeper somehow. Our mouths didn't open; our tongues didn't entwine. It was a simple kiss on the lips, and yet it felt so sincere, so honest, and so much like what love must be like, that it left me breathless.

When he pulled his lips off mine, he smiled as he looked into my eyes and I caressed his cheek. "You're a very nice guy, Cash Gentry. Most men wouldn't want to kiss lips that are busted and swollen."

"Well, most men haven't had the pleasure of kissing your lips when they're in prime condition. If they had, then they would know, without a doubt, that lips like yours make for good kissing even when they're beat up." He kissed me once more, making my heart feel wiggly.

"Oh, yeah?" came my stupid response. But the fact was, he had me feeling a little drunk on his small kisses.

"Yeah." He ran his finger along my nose, making me feel all cute and adorable as he looked at me. "And I think tonight I'll give you a nice hot bath, a back rub, and some TLC to help ease the pain your body has to be in."

I'd played off the pain the whole night. Now, I didn't feel like I should anymore. He wanted to pamper me—why not let him? "A hot bath sounds great. You getting in too?"

"Hell yes I am." Sliding his arm along the seat behind me, he draped it around my shoulders as he pulled away from the now dark and quiet bar.

I leaned my head on his shoulder as he drove us to his place. "So, I get to spend the night, huh?"

"Get to?" he asked. "No, you have to. I'm not about to let you go back home tonight. And not tomorrow night either. And then we've got our plans for Sunday and Monday, so you'll be with me for those nights too."

"That's four nights." I hadn't ever stayed away from home that long. "And I'll have to go home in the morning to pack."

"I'm loaded, baby. I'll buy you everything you need." He kissed my cheek. "It's the least I can do for my little boxer."

His boxer. His baby. His. I like the way that sounds all of a sudden.

CHAPTER FIFTEEN

Cash

I'd never had a girl fight over me before. And the way Bobbi Jo looked, she'd fought like a Viking over me. And over just one little kiss too. She had it bad for me. I knew that then.

No matter how much we'd told each other that it wasn't serious, and that we were free agents, it was beginning to sink in with both of us just how much we actually cared about each other.

After parking the truck in the garage, I led Bobbi Jo into the house through the kitchen. "Have you eaten today?" I had my doubts.

"I had an egg sandwich for breakfast, but nothing after that. And by breakfast, I mean around noon." She ran her hand over her stomach. "I could use a bite."

I loved that about the girl. She wasn't afraid to let me know when she was hungry. "Let's see what we've got in the fridge."

She went to take a seat at the island bar as I rummaged through the fridge. "Anything will be fine. I'm not going to be picky."

I pulled out a jar of pickles. "How about a sandwich?"

With a nod, she said, "I said *anything* will be fine, Cash."

"You want some milk with it?" I got out the almond milk as she nodded.

In no time at all, I had a little plate with a couple of turkey sandwiches, pickles, and potato chips, along with two glasses of milk. I sat next to her, then we dug in.

Sitting there in the dim light of the kitchen, the only light on being the one under the cabinets, I liked how we could sit in silence, eating, not thinking about what to say or how to act.

After finishing, she picked up our plates and cleaned things up as I sat there watching her. "We make a good team, Bobbi Jo."

"We do, don't we?" she asked as she put the dirty dishes into the dishwasher. "Maybe you and I should start a business together. You know, do something worthwhile."

"Anything but a bar," I said as I got up when she walked toward me. Putting my arm around her shoulders, I started heading to my room. "These late nights aren't good for us to be doing so much."

"You sound like an old man." She laughed as we went up the stairs.

"What I really mean is that if we ended our nights earlier, then we'd be getting into bed a lot earlier. And once in bed, we could get it on a lot earlier and do it a lot longer." I smiled at her as we topped the stairs.

"Oh, now I get it. It's all about sex to you." She smacked me on the shoulder.

"Of course." I was kidding and she knew that. "And cuddling too. Don't forget cuddling."

"How could I forget the cuddling?" She walked into my bedroom as I opened the door for her. "What a gentleman you are, Cash Gentry."

"I am pretty gentleman-like with you, aren't I?" I'd never been a total ass or anything like that with women before, but with Bobbi Jo, I tended to do a lot more for her.

As I closed the door, she went to toward the bathroom. "I'm going to peel these clothes off while you make me that hot bath you promised. My body is aching."

At least she was finally admitting how much she hurt. "I'm about to fix you all up, Rocky."

She stopped just inside the bathroom door, then turned to look at me as she began pulling off her clothes. "Look, I'm kind of regretting what I did. Maybe lay off the boxer nicknames. I think I need to apologize to my sister. I mean, she deserved a smack or even two, but I gave her a beatdown. I don't know if she needed all that."

"Bet she doesn't try to trick me anymore." I grinned as I moved past her to go start the huge jet tub.

She laughed. "Bet she doesn't try to kiss you anymore, that's for sure. But still, I went overboard."

"I guess you're in love with me," I said, knowing I was pushing it.

"Or, more likely, I'm sick of her doing this to guys I like. It's been years and years. Maybe I finally got fed up with it once and for all. My mind snapped this time." She looked at the half-full tub, standing there naked. "Can I get in yet?"

"I guess so." I started to strip down as she climbed into the tub. "It'll have to get deeper before I can turn on the jets though."

"I don't care." She eased back, her eyes closing. "It's hot and wonderful already. I so needed this." She opened her eyes to look at me as I dropped my jeans. "I so need you."

With the last article of clothing off my body, I got in, sliding in behind her. She leaned back on me, and I ran my hand through her hair. "I like this."

"Me too." She hummed as I rubbed her shoulders.

Feeling relaxed with her, I asked, "Do you ever see yourself settling down?"

"Not for a very long time." She ran her hands down my thighs, leaving them resting on my knees. "I like my life. Well, mostly I do. And now that I have you as a very pleasant distraction, it's even better. Why try to settle down now?"

"I don't know. I just mean that this pace, this working five nights a week is—well, it's not easy." I'd wanted to have a more normal relationship, and with her working at the bar, it wasn't falling into place easily.

"Is that why you ate lunch with my sister today?" she asked as I felt her tense up a bit. "Because I'm not really accessible until after three in the afternoon?"

"I honestly didn't think about that. I asked her to join me so I could get to know more about *you*, if you want the truth." I didn't know a whole hell of a lot about Bobbi Jo. Our time was limited, and usually, lots of people were around. It made it difficult to get to know her on a personal level.

"Well, never think you should get any information about me from her again." She turned her head to one side to look at me from the corner of her eye. "Just ask me anything you want to know."

"Okay then. What's your favorite color? What do you like to do when you have time off? What kind of food is your favorite?" I had a load of questions for her.

She held up one hand. "Stop." A long sigh filled the gap. "Blue, like your eyes. Sleep. And pizza."

I kissed the top of her head as I kept rubbing her shoulders. "Do you want to ask me anything?"

"What is your opinion on mixed vegetables? You know that can of them that you get in the store?" she asked.

I had no idea what to say to that. I had no opinion on something like that at all. "Are you being serious?"

"Very." She turned all the way over, her breasts pressed against my chest, our bodies flush underneath the water. "I need to know if we are really compatible. Now, you may think you have no opinion, but everyone does. If you are served mixed veggies, how does it make you feel? Do you eat them the way they are? Do you separate them into piles of green beans, corn, and carrots? Or do you simply not eat them at all?"

I had to think about it for a moment. The concept had never come to my mind before. But finally, I knew how I felt about the food. "I don't like mixed veggies. If I wanted all of them mixed up, I would mix them up myself. Like, why have one can of them like that when you can get individual cans? What if you like green beans but hate carrots? What if you just want corn? So, I am against mixed vegetables."

Her eyes lit up, as did her body. "I've never been more attracted to you, Cash Gentry."

"So, that's how you feel too?" I asked.

She nodded. "I hate them and I never want to have even a single can of them in my home whenever I get one of my own. My mother has an entire shelf of the nasty things. I could never even think of being serious with a man who has no opinion on mixed vegetables."

"So, I *am* a prospect then?" I had to smile at her as she slid up my body.

Her hand on my hard cock told me she was rather enthused about this find she'd made in me. "Oh, yeah. You're a prospect all right." She moved her body until she had me inside of her. A long moan escaped her as she settled on top of me. "Think we'll make a mess if we do this in the tub?"

"Definitely." I lifted her up then let her slide back down my long, hard cock. "But who the hell cares. Ride me, baby."

She put her hands on my shoulders to hang on. "Buck."

Moving up with sharp thrusts, I had her whimpering with desire as I held her by the waist. "Oh, you're about to get the ride of your life."

"Give it to me, cowboy," she moaned. "Give it to me good. Make me hang on for dear life."

"You had better hang on. I'm about to blow you out of the water." I moved hard and fast, watching her tits bounce as water splashed around us like tidal waves.

She reached behind me to hit the button to make the jets turn on. Water pounded my back as I moved and she squealed with delight. Hearing her sexy laugh as we romped around made me feel something I never had before.

I felt happy just to be with her. If all we were doing was watching television, I had a feeling I'd still be happy. She made me happy in a way no one ever had.

Her body went tight; her nails dug into shoulders. "Cash!" She came all over my hard cock, her walls quaking around me, squeezing me.

I moved us, turning her over, getting behind her, then thrusting into her still pulsing pussy as I pounded into her from behind. My jaw tight, my hands on her waist, holding her steady as I thrusted into her hard, over and over. Water moved in waves, sloshing over the edges, spilling onto the tiled floor.

Everything combined to make it one of the hottest times we'd ever had. When I felt the urge to let it all go, she screamed and came again. "Cash! Damn! Fuck!"

I had no choice; she pulled it from me. I gave it all to her, filling her with my hot seed. "Baby, damn!"

She'd taken me to a whole other place with that orgasm. All I wanted was to go there again and again.

CHAPTER SIXTEEN

Bobbi Jo

Soft snores met my ears as I woke up. Cash's arms around my body made me smile. The wetness between my legs made me stop smiling. "Shit."

Why would there be wetness between my legs when we used a condom?

The activities from the night before came drifting back into my mind. The bath, the bed, the floor, the walk-in closet—and all those times and places had one thing in common.

No condom.

It took me a second to realize I wasn't breathing. When I gasped, the noise made Cash stir a little. I didn't move, didn't take another breath.

I had to get the hell out of there. Maybe I could find a morning-after pill. I had to do something to rectify my reckless behavior.

Sneaking out of the bed, moving his arm a little at a time, I was able to move away from him. Going to the bathroom, with my goal being to find my clothes and put them back on, I went to pee first.

Rubbing my temples, I tried to think about what the right thing to do was. I'd never come out and told Cash that I didn't take any type of birth control. All I had said was that he needed to use a condom. But lots of girls made guys use condoms even if they were on birth control. They did that to protect themselves from getting STDs. And for all I knew, that was what Cash thought too. He apparently didn't think we *had* to use them, or he would've made sure to use them last night.

And what about last night? What the hell happened to me? Why had I forgotten all about using protection?

Maybe I'd taken a punch to the head that I wasn't aware of. That kind of thing could happen. Maybe I was just out of it and didn't even realize it. And now I'd gone and had sex a whole lot in one night.

I counted the times I could recall on my fingers. Four in all—and none of them with a condom and all had ended with me getting blasted with baby juice.

I'd never wished harder that I had brought my own car so I could just leave. But there was a cab service I could call, so I made that my plan. Only I had no idea what the address to Cash's mansion was.

Just as I got off the toilet and walked over to the sink to use the toothbrush Cash had given me the first night I'd slept over, I heard the sound of the door opening and in came Cash—naked and rubbing his head. "Morning, sweet thing."

"Um, yeah. Hi." I put some toothpaste on my toothbrush then began scrubbing the crap off my teeth as if that would eradicate the abundance of semen that had been squirted at my eggs.

"Hi?" He laughed as he took a piss, still scratching his head with his free hand.

Spitting out the toothpaste, I grabbed the mouthwash. "You know, I was thinking that I could just call a cab and go back home this morning." The idea of stopping at a pharmacy to see about getting that pill to erase the previous night's mistakes was at the top of my mind.

"Nope." He came up behind me, running his arms around my waist, nuzzling my neck. He whispered, "You're staying with me, remember? And for now, we're going to get right back into that warm bed where I'm going to kiss you, hug you, and make love to you until we fall back to sleep."

Him, all up on me like that, made me want to do just what he'd said. Only I knew I had to get to town and to a pharmacy. "That's so sweet sounding."

"Oh, there's not going to be anything sweet about it." He pushed his already hard cock against my bare ass. "See."

"So, right to it, then?" I shook my head. "No, I can't. Sorry."

Being that neither of us had a stitch on, he pulled me toward the shower. "I get it. You feel dirty. We can do it in the shower."

"I've already got quite a bit of love juices on me already, that is true." I would need to, at the very least, rinse off. A full body scrub, inside and out, would've been best, but I had no idea if I had the time for that.

"I'll clean us all up," he said as he pushed the button to start the jets spraying all over the place. Pulling me in with him, he placed me on the tiled seat then grabbed a bar of soap, lathering his hands as his hair became drenched and hung down past his broad shoulders.

I couldn't speak as he moved those soapy hands all over my body. The way he moved around me had me feeling lightheaded again, tipsy even. "I like waking up with you in my arms, Bobbi Jo. I was disappointed when I woke up to find you gone."

"You were?" My head lolled back as he massaged my tits.

I felt his lips on one nipple. "I was very disappointed."

"Maybe you're getting a little too spoiled." I groaned as he sucked on the nipple, licking it as he did.

"Maybe." He kissed a trail down my stomach then pushed my knees apart to spread my legs open. "Let me get you all cleaned up."

I didn't see what his attention to me down there could hurt. There was time after all. I slightly remembered that the pill I'd heard about could be used up to forty-eight hours after intercourse. I had plenty of time. "Please do."

His soapy hands moved all over my pussy that was swollen from all the pounding he'd done to it during our night's activities. "You're so ready for me, baby." His lips pressed against my clit and I gasped with how amazing it felt. "If you think that feels good, wait until I really give you a sweet, long kiss."

I had to grip his shoulders as he kissed me harder down there, his tongue moving all around in ways that seemed impossible. "Cash!"

He didn't stop. He thrust his tongue into me, pushing it in and out until I was screaming his name, a thing he absolutely loved. His fingers dug into my thighs as he couldn't seem to get enough of what I was giving him.

When he pulled back, he looked at me with wild eyes, then I was on my knees on the shower floor as he took me from behind. All I could hear was the sound of the shower jets pouring water over our bodies and the slapping of skin.

I should've said something about protection then. I knew I should've said something. But I didn't want to stop what we were doing. I didn't want to ruin the moment.

When I felt the heat fill me, his cock jerking hard inside of me as he grunted and groaned, I knew I had a whole new batch of baby soup inside of me.

My body sagged as I sighed, then he slapped my ass playfully. "Now that's the right way to start your day. Huh, little momma?"

Little momma?

"Cash, I want to tell you something." He pulled me up and held me tight in his arms, his mouth on mine stopping my words and my train of thought.

The next thing I knew, we weren't in the shower anymore. The bed was under my back when he laid me down on it, then he was on top of me, back inside of me and we were right back at it.

I had no idea what had gotten into the man, but he was letting it all out into me. Over and over. And I couldn't find it in myself to say a word to stop him from doing it either.

For some reason, I was as wrapped up in him as he was in me. And when exhaustion finally took us both over, we crashed on his bed, our bodies all tangled up together, him still inside of me, and we fell asleep.

Somewhere in the deep recesses of my mind, I told myself that I would definitely get up later, go to the pharmacy and get that pill. It would eradicate all we'd done. Everything would be just fine.

Sleep took me over. Hours later, when I felt Cash moving behind me, getting off the bed, I opened my eyes as he said, "Shit. Babe, get up. We've got to get you down to the bar. It's only thirty minutes until it's supposed to open. I'll get Tyrell to see if Ella has something you can borrow to wear to work."

"We slept all day?" I didn't feel like that was possible.

"Apparently. Come on, now. Shake a leg, girl."

Hurrying, I felt dizzy and then realized I hadn't eaten or drank anything all day. "Damn, Cash, I feel like I might pass out."

He nodded as he turned the shower on. "Just get in here and let's not mess around. We've got to get going."

Rushing around, somehow we both got dressed. I found Ella had left me some jeans and a T-shirt on the bed. I'd met her only once and was appreciative of her help. "Remind me to do something nice for Ella for lending me her clothes. It was nice of her."

"Yeah, yeah. Come on." Cash grabbed my hand and away we went. Into the garage where he lifted me up into his truck and then we sped away to the bar.

Being a Saturday night, there were already three cars in the parking lot when we pulled up. I had to get right to work and the night was nothing but chaos for the most part.

When my sister came in the door, her hair in her very made-up face, I took a second. Wiggling my finger, I led her to the back. "Look, I went too far."

Betty Sue pulled her hair back, and I could still see the black around her eyes, the swelling of her nose and mouth, and the chunk of hair that I'd yanked out. "You think?"

"Did Dad see you?" I prayed like hell that she hadn't gone and told on me.

"No. I stayed in bed ... claimed I was sick." She sighed. "I shouldn't have done what I did. Although it wasn't exactly planned out for me to get a kiss from Cash, I didn't do anything the right way. None of it. And I am sorry for that."

"And I'm sorry I laid into you so hard. We're adults; we could've handled it like adults." I put my hand on her shoulder. "Let's put this behind us, shall we?"

She nodded. "I've been thinking that this whole time. We need to put all this behind us. All the past years of me doing things to you that have hurt you and you never retaliated. Well, there was that one time you nearly killed me with the laxative. But mostly, you just took what I did and did nothing back to me. I figure that beating you put on me was justified."

I was relieved that she felt that way. But I knew I'd gone too far. "Two wrongs don't make a right. I'll make it up to you, Betty Sue."

She held up her hand, putting it on my chest. "No, you won't. We're even now. Let's move on from here and let all that go. I can see that you really care about Cash. And he must really care about you too. I think he does, anyway. He's a good man, Bobbi Jo. Don't do anything dumb and let him go or let him let you go either."

Before I could say anything, Cash walked into the back room. He smiled as he saw us together. "Good. You two have kissed and made up. That's nice to see." He came up and wrapped his big arms around us both. "We can let bygones be bygones now." When he backed up, taking his arms off us, he looked at my sister. "I'm taking Bobbi Jo out of town tomorrow. We won't be back until Monday night. Think you can tell your parents about that, so they don't have to worry?"

She nodded. "I can do that." Then she looked at me. "He's a good one, sister. Don't lose him."

Before I could say a thing, Cash said, "I won't let her lose me."

All I could do was stare at the man. *What the hell is going on here?*

CHAPTER SEVENTEEN

Cash

The night had been crazy at the bar even with me helping out. But I had managed to find some time to make arrangements for our little getaway.

Even though I hadn't ever done anything like this before, I was smart enough to ask the lady who ran the travel agency in town for help. She'd come in with her husband for a few drinks and a game of pool. With her help, not only did I have all the accommodations taken care of, I had everything Bobbi Jo would need already packed away on the private jet that waited for us at the Carthage Municipal Airport.

"This is silly," Bobbi Jo argued as I drove straight to the airport, passing up the road to her house. "I can just stop by and pack a bag real quick."

"I can see you won't give up, so I'll just go ahead and tell you." I put my arm around her, giving her a squeeze. "I've got everything you need already on the plane. We both do."

She huffed as if she didn't believe me. "And how did you accomplish this, Cash?"

"I had help." I knew she'd be flabbergasted when she saw all I had accomplished while working so hard with her at the bar. "And you and I really should think about starting a business together. Maybe we'll come up with something in the next couple of days."

Her lips quirked up to one side in a lopsided grin. "If you can keep your hands off of me for long enough for our brains to work."

"Well, maybe we won't come up with something." I kissed her cheek. I had no intentions of keeping my hands off her. "We've got nothing but time, girl."

Parking the truck at the airport in the dark of night, I watched Bobbi Jo's eyes light up when the door to the plane's hanger was raised, and the shiny black plane came into view. "Is that it?"

"It has Whisper Ranch written on the side of it," I pointed out. "I think it's a pretty safe bet to think that is it."

I got out of the truck then caught her as she slid out of it too. "It's so beautiful."

"Wait until you see the inside." I had big plans for her inside that plane. "There's a bedroom in there."

She sucked in her breath. "There can't be."

"There is. Right in the back of the plane. And a bathroom too." I took her hand, leading her to the plane where the pilot came out to greet us.

"I hear we're heading to Maine for some lobster." He shook my hand. "Nice to see you again, Cash. And this must be Miss Bobbi Jo Baker. I'm Steven. It's a pleasure to be your pilot this evening." He looked at his watch. "Or rather, this morning. We'll be in Biddeford, Maine in a little over five hours. It's three a.m. now, so that means—"

Bobbi Jo chimed in, "Around ten in the morning. Wait. No, they're ahead of us. Around eleven a.m. we'll be there."

Steven nodded. "Just in time for lunch. And the lobster at Docks Boathouse is off the charts. You'll love it and the atmosphere. Even if it is near freezing."

I hadn't thought about how damn cold it would be in Maine in early February. Texas never had it that damn bad. "Maybe we should go in the other direction."

Steven shook his head. "Nah. We'll be great going that way. And you can't get any better lobster than you can in Maine. So, climb aboard and let's get this party going, shall we? After lunch in Maine, we're going to New York City so you two can stay the night at the Waldorf."

Bobbi Jo's eyes went wide. "Oh, no. Cash, I don't have a clue what to wear. I don't know. This is too much."

"Relax." I tugged her to come with me up the stairs to get on the plane. "I told you: someone else has packed all we'll need for our little trip. It'll be fun. You'll see. But first, you've got to chill, girl."

Taking our seats in the cabin, we put on the seatbelts as Steven got the plane going. Bobbi Jo looked at me with a nervous expression. "I've never been on a plane."

"It's nothing to be worried about." I held her hand then pulled it up to kiss it. "I've got ya. And there are parachutes in the overhead bins."

"Have you ever used one before?" she asked me with a doubtful expression.

"No." But I knew I could do it if I had to. "Believe me: if this plane is going down, I'm going to figure out how to leave it before it hits the ground."

"Cash, I'm going to need to get some sleep with all you've planned." She cut her eyes at the door at the back of the cabin, the one that led to the bedroom. "If we go back there, all we're going to do is sleep. Got me?"

I did have mile-high plans for her. But there was always the trip back home. "I got ya, sweet thing."

With a smile, she closed her eyes. "I've never even dreamt of doing anything like this. It's out of this world amazing."

"And it hasn't even really started yet." I loved the fact that I could do this for her and with her. "Just to let you know, there's never been anyone I've wanted to do something this out of my element with. I must really trust you, Bobbi Jo."

"I must really trust you too, Cash. There isn't anyone else I would've agreed to go with on a trip like this." She sighed. "But I think you're safe enough."

With the plane taking off, we both closed our eyes, and soon we were both sleeping the remainder of the night away. The sun coming up woke us both up and what I saw out the small window took my breath away. "Wow, that's gorgeous."

Bobbi Jo nodded and stretched. "Up here, the way we are, it looks so different—so majestic."

Unbuckling my seatbelt, I thought we should go back to the bedroom and see about getting ready for the day. "Come on; let's go see what we've got back here."

She came along. "So, I have to ask how you managed to get all this done so quickly."

"I'm magic," I said as I opened the door. There were two suitcases on the bed, both open and both empty. "And it seems the person who packed our bags must've unpacked them for us too."

She went to the closet and gasped. "Look at these clothes. There's a black suit for you." Her eyes were big as she read the label. "Are you kidding me?"

"It's some expensive designer, isn't it?" I shook my head as I thought how uncomfortable that was going to be.

"Well, it's just Ralph Lauren, but it looks like something James Bond would wear." She pulled out a dark blue dress. "And look what I'm supposed to wear."

"You will look gorgeous in that dress." I already pictured her wearing it.

"No way." She put it back. "That's so not me."

"Well, the suit is so not me too. But I am going to wear it while we're in New York at that fancy hotel and you will wear the dress. It's beautiful." I went to take her in my arms. "Almost as beautiful as you are."

"But it's so, well, so girly." She frowned. "It's just not me."

"While in New York, one should do what they do. Come on. It'll be like playing dress-up when you were a kid." I kissed her on top of her head. "Now let's shower, then we'll put on something that's casual that I'm sure they've packed for us. For the next two days, you and I are going to be out of our elements, and we're going to see how the other half lives."

She blinked at me a few times. "Only *you* are a part of the other half now, Cash. You're a billionaire."

"And you're with me." I kissed her lips. "Come on. Let's forget about who we really are and be whatever we want to be. At least for a couple of days. I've never been able to do anything like this. I've never even thought to wish for something like this. And I'm damn glad I've got you with me to do it."

She smiled. "I'm glad I'm here with you too. It's weird, but a fun weird."

"If you play your cards right, you'll get to do lots more of this kind of thing with me." I led her to the bathroom where we could shower.

"Who said I'm even playing cards, Cash?" She laughed as I turned to start taking her clothes off.

"Okay, neither of us are playing cards at this time. It's just fun being with each other, don't you think?"

She nodded as I pulled the shirt off over her head. "It is fun being with you, Cash."

"And it's fun being with you, Bobbi Jo." I really did hope we could find something to do together to get her out of that bar. "Maybe we'll find out that we want to open a seafood restaurant in Carthage after eating this lobster."

Her mouth dropped open. "That's actually a great idea. But we might find something even better than that. Running a restaurant is no joke. That takes tons of time."

I thought spending tons of time with her might be a great way to spend time. But she was right. A restaurant would be a lot of hard work, and I figured one would need a fair amount of passion for food to run one anyway.

"Maybe we'll do something a little different, a little less work and a lot more fun." I finished undressing her, kissing her bare shoulder.

"Oh, I know what we could open: a skating rink. My parents use to talk about going to one when they were in their teens. They said it was the local hangout." She began taking my clothes off. "We could do it all old-school—nostalgic, you know."

My lips quirked up to one side. "I like that idea."

"Plus, it won't be open late." She pulled my shirt off, running her hands over my pecs. "And it'll be a good exercise for people too."

I took her hands in mine, holding them to my heart. "That is a great idea, Bobbi Jo." Maybe we would find a way to spend our time together that didn't include nights at a bar.

CHAPTER EIGHTEEN

Bobbi Jo

"So this is it—the East Coast." I stared out at the battleship gray water with small white peaks that floated on top. "I always thought the Atlantic Ocean was a bit more—well, majestic."

"This is just a bay," some man said who came up behind Cash and me as we stood on the dock just outside the restaurant. "Believe me—the Atlantic *is* a sight to behold."

"I'm sure it is," Cash said. "Come on, Bobbi Jo. Let's head inside to get something to eat."

By the way he looked at me out of the corner of his eye, I thought he might have been embarrassed by what I'd said. "It's just that I went to the gulf coast once when I was younger, and that water was gorgeous. Like emerald green, clear, and the sand was this really clean light beige color. Now *that* was pretty." I held my arm out in a gesture to our surroundings. "*This*, not so much."

Now Cash had a frown on his face as he looked at me. "Bobbi Jo, can it, will ya?"

I supposed he was worried about offending the locals, so I shut up. The one thing that saved it all were the lobsters. Cash pointed at the mountain of them that sat on a platter on the counter. "Whoa, look at those."

"Now that is a sight to behold." My mouth already watered to taste at least three of them.

With bibs in place, Cash and I began chowing down on the delicious seafood feast that was spread out in front of us. "You want some more butter?" he asked as he pushed a bowl of it toward me.

I dipped a chunk of white lobster into it. "Yes, please." I saw no possible way that we'd be able to walk out of the place. We'd need wheelbarrows to get us back out the door we'd come in through.

An hour and a half later, we waddled outside. The car that had brought us from the airport was still waiting with our suitcases in the trunk to take us to New York. "Here we go, Bobbi Jo." Cash let me get in first.

He and I leaned on one another as the car drove off. Once again, we fell asleep on the ride; it was beginning to be our thing. Get into a moving vehicle—crash out.

The late nights seemed to be catching up with both of us. And the hours and hours of sex probably had a hand in it too.

"We're here," came the driver's voice. "I'll give your baggage to the porter. You two can go in and check in."

I felt like Dorothy in the *Wizard of Oz*. "Where are we?"

"New York," the driver said. "The Waldorf Astoria."

People were everywhere. I could have sworn that there were more people around us than we had in the entire town of Carthage. "I never knew so many people could be in one place at the same time. It seems impossible."

"We're from Texas," Cash let the driver know. "This is like another planet to us."

The door opened, and a man in what looked like a suit one would wear in England at the Queen's palace stood there. "Welcome to the Waldorf Astoria. Please come with me."

Cash and I exchanged nervous glances then got out of the car. Standing up, breathing in the same air as all those around us, felt weird. "Oh, man. I don't know about this, Cash."

"Come on, Bobbi Jo." He pulled me along with him. "It's going to be fun."

"It's going to be something all right. I don't know about fun, but it will be something." I wasn't so sure this place was for me. I wasn't an uptown girl. Not that I was a country bumpkin, but I wasn't a city girl either. "You know, I've never known this about Carthage, but for a town, it's more like the country. I'm way out of my element here, Cash."

He stopped and looked at me with a stern look on his face. "You have got to stop talking like that. If you can't say anything good, just try not to say anything. Please."

For the first time ever, I could feel the difference between Cash and myself. He was rich. He might not have always known he was, but it ran in his veins. He held his head high as we walked up to the front desk. "Gentry—reservation for two."

"Oh, yes. Everything has been taken care of." The woman who stood behind the desk was quick to summon a bellhop. "Take our guests up to room five-thirty-four." She waved at the man who had our luggage on a golden cart. "Give those to him, please. He'll see them up to their suite."

Cash reached into his pocket, pulling out some money, then handed the porter some. "Thank you."

I held onto Cash's other hand, wondering when he had the time to grow sophisticated. I hadn't found that time yet. "You seem like you've done this before."

His lips pressed against the shell of my ear. "Of course I've never done this before. But I have watched movies. Haven't you?"

Shrugging, I had never cared for movies about New York or any other fancy crap. "Not really."

I stayed quiet all the way up to our room. Once inside, I had to put my hand over my mouth as I was afraid my stupid would pour out some more. But after the bellhop left us, a generous tip in his hand, I had to blurt it out, "This place is like something out of a Hemingway novel." I ran to the window and looked out at the buildings, the people, and all the traffic. "It's insanity out there."

When I turned back around, I saw Cash wearing another frown. "Bobbi Jo, what's with you? I never saw this coming. You are acting like—for lack of a better phrase—a country mouse."

Throwing up my hands, I didn't know how he wanted me to act. "Should I be pretending that I've ever seen anything like this? Should I be acting as if I've always been snobbish, semi-royalty? And why are you acting like this is old hat to you, Cash?"

"Maybe it's because I grew up in Dallas, I don't know." He took a seat on a chair that would've been deemed too fancy to sit on back home. "But this isn't all that out of the ordinary to me. I mean, well, of course, it's different and large, crowded, and even sort of odd-feeling. But the thing is, it's still just a place, Bobbi Jo. You're acting like we've landed on another planet."

He'd hit the nail on the head. "Yes, that's exactly what it feels like to me. And you seem to be acclimating to the atmosphere quite easily while I am having difficulty with it."

His eyes scanned the room, landing on the minibar. "Maybe a drink would chill you out."

"You know I don't drink." I went to sit on the bed and found it hard as a rock. "Ow." I slapped my hand on the mattress. "This thing is so hard."

He came and sat down beside me. "Well, it's not hard, just firm. I suppose people around here like their mattresses firmer than we do in Texas."

"I don't think this trip is turning out the way we'd hoped." I got up then went to look around at the rest of the room.

"You might think about giving it a chance, Bobbi Jo." Cash looked grim. "We could take a nap, I guess. Maybe you've got jetlag."

"Why do you think that?" I put my hands on my hips. "Because I like Texas better than New York, I've got jetlag? Maybe I just happen to like my home better than you do."

His eyes rolled. "Maybe I just shouldn't have brought you here. Maybe a trip to the Dairy King would've been more your speed."

"I didn't ask you to do this, Cash." He was pissing me off by acting like I was some ingrate who'd asked him to do this for me. "You came up with this whole idea. Do you want me to lie? Do you want me to pretend that I love the crowds, the noise, the bone-chilling cold?" I ran my hands up and down my arms. "What is with this cold anyway? It's wet and sticky. And quite frankly, the air smells weird here."

He fell back on the bed, sighing heavily. "I need a nap. Maybe you should take a shower and get yourself ready to go eat later."

"I'm not even remotely hungry yet." I went back to sit in the fancy chair he'd vacated. "Is there anywhere comfortable to sit in this whole room?"

Cash sat back up and looked at me with a bewildered expression. "Do you have any idea how much this room costs?"

I shrugged. "I hope it's not a lot. It's not worth it."

"It *is* a lot. And people come from all over the world to stay here. People feel appreciative of staying here, in this hotel which is known all over the globe." He fell back and sighed again. "How did I not know this about you?"

"How did I not know that you were a closet rich guy?" I got up and went to see what was in the little bar. "I need a Dr. Pepper." When I opened it, I saw many things inside. "There's some type of water in here that I've never seen before. And some club soda too. But guess what there isn't any of?"

"Dr. Pepper," Cash said, sounding weary.

"Yeah. How in the hell do they not have Dr. Pepper?" I was stupefied.

"Can't you just pick something else in there, Bobbi Jo? It's not like you only drink that one soda." He turned over on his side to look at me. "And may I recommend, once again, a real drink. You're kind of being a jackass. Pretty much since we landed, you've had nothing nice to say."

"I beg your pardon." I'd loved the lunch we'd had. "I had only nice things to say about Docks Boathouse. Now that place is one for the books. I have never tasted fresher seafood in my life. I would definitely come back just to eat there. Even if the water wasn't as pretty as I had thought it would be."

"Well, you haven't eaten here yet. Maybe the food here will make this place worth your while." He rolled over, putting his back to me.

As I stood there, looking at him, I thought about how different we were. "You know, my parents haven't ever had a lot of money, Cash."

"Mine neither," he said quietly.

"I suppose I just never thought I would even come to New York or the East Coast." I hadn't ever traveled much at all. "Have you ever been out of Texas?" I went to sit on the bed next to him, running my hand over his back.

"No, I haven't ever been out of Texas, Bobbi Jo." He rolled over to look at me. "This is my first trip out of state. This is my first time to see anything, other than a Texas sky—anything other than a Texas city."

I gulped as I saw something in his eyes I'd never seen before. "You have that thing you see in men's eyes who are wealthy and powerful, Cash. I've never seen it there before, but now I can see it clearly. You're going to outgrow me."

The way he stared into my eyes only cemented that fact in my mind and in my heart too.

CHAPTER NINETEEN

Cash

The trip out of town told me more about Bobbi Jo than all our time in the sack. The remainder of our stay in New York wasn't any better than how it had begun.

She hated the meal at the Waldorf. She hated wearing the dress she'd found on the plane. She hated the bed we had to sleep on in the hotel. She hated the breakfast of lox and bagels. She hated the whole thing.

So, when we got back to Carthage, I decided to give it a rest. Maybe she and I didn't have such a great connection after all. I couldn't say I saw it coming, but I had known that she was a small-town girl and, apparently, she wanted to stay that way.

A month had passed since I'd seen her. When I drove through town in the evenings, I saw her car at The Watering Hole. She was still tending bar, which I figured she might do for the rest of her life.

I sat in a booth at the Dairy King one afternoon when my brother's wife came to sit down with me. Tiffany's family owned the small café, and she had been there helping out. "Hey, you. Why do you look so down in the dumps?"

"Do I look that bad?" I hadn't realized I was that transparent.

She nodded. "You've been looking this way for a while now. So, I'm done waiting to find out why that is. You're going to have to tell me."

"I guess I just don't know what I want in a woman. I mean, I want someone who's down to Earth and stuff like that, but I want someone who wants to see the world too." I didn't know if there was anyone out there like that.

"I don't see what the problem in that is." She looked at me with a puzzled expression. "I thought you and Bobbi Jo from the bar were getting along well. What happened with her?"

"I took her to New York."

When Tiffany nodded as if she understood, I wondered what it was about New York that had Texas women so thrown off. "Well, taking her so far off and to such a different place than Carthage was risky. See, she's been here all her life. I don't know a whole lot about her or her family, but I do know they're from pretty humble beginnings. That might've been way too fancy for her just yet."

"I'm going to want a woman to go places with me. I want to travel the world, Tiff. I want to see it all." I hadn't ever known that about myself, but now I knew it.

"Maybe she's not the right woman for you then, Cash."

Just her saying that made me mad. "But what if she is? What if she's the right woman and I'll just have to suck it up and not get to live my dream?"

Looking confused, she asked, "When did this become your dream, Cash?"

"After that trip." I sighed. "I wanted to really enjoy everything but couldn't because Bobbi Jo had to bitch about it all. The one thing she did like was the lobster place. That was it. Out of everything I took her to do, that was it."

"Okay, see it wasn't a complete bust then." She pulled out her cell. "There are lots of places you can go that might have more of what you both want to do."

"Hell, we haven't even talked in over a month. I doubt she'd give me the time of day anymore." I knew it had bothered her that I hadn't called or come by since we got back to Carthage. I waved at her once when we passed each other in the street, and she'd given me the middle finger wave.

"Why haven't you talked, Cash?" Tiffany reached over to put her hand on the back of mine, as I had it lying on the table. "Did she do anything that bad while you were on the trip that warranted you not talking to her?"

"No." *She just didn't have a good time.* "It's just that it was the first trip I've ever taken out of the state. And to be honest, she's the first girl I've ever even taken on a trip anywhere. I thought it would be different. I thought she was more like me."

"But you didn't even know you wanted to travel until recently, right?" she asked.

"Yeah." I looked out the window. "But things are different now. I mean, I just don't know what I want anymore."

"You want that small-town girl, Cash. But you want her to be something she's not. That's not real fair, is it?"

I shook my head. "Nope."

I heard the phone ring up at the counter, and when the girl said Bobbi Jo's name, I knew she was calling in her nightly order. Tiffany did too as she looked over her shoulder at the girl who'd taken the order. "Hey, I'll get that out to Bobbi Jo. Let me know when it's ready." She looked back at me. "And by me, I mean you're taking it to her."

"She might not want to talk to me." I had been thinking it had been kind of shallow of me to just stop talking to her over something kind of dumb. "Dumping her just because she didn't like where we went isn't a good reason, is it?"

"Not really. And you two are young, Cash. She may not be ready to see the world just yet, but maybe one day she will be. You just moved too fast, went too far, you know?" Tiff got up as the girl put the bag of food on the counter and nodded at her. "Come on, Cash. Time to make up. I'm not saying you've got to start seeing her again, but at least make up."

"I don't know." But even as I said that, I got up to follow her. "I do miss talking to her. And kissing her."

Tiffany handed the bag of food to me. "Cash, there's more to a relationship than just the kissing. Maybe you and Bobbi Jo should spend some time doing things that aren't sex-related. Maybe getting to know one another better would be a nice change of pace."

"I wasn't looking to get serious." I walked toward the door. "How did it get serious when I wasn't trying for that?"

She shrugged. "Sometimes things just get out of control. Don't ask her out. Don't try to kiss her. Just give her the food. Tell her you took care of her tab—which I'm going to tear up right now—and then I want you to ask her how her night is going. Ask her how she's been. Let her know you miss her."

"Ugh!" I walked out, then went to get into the truck. "How did things get this way?"

As I drove to the bar, I saw an empty lot, and it caught my eye for the first time. I'd looked up old skating rinks and thought one would fit pretty good right there. But I wasn't going to say a thing about it to Bobbi Jo.

She and I were on different pages of our lives, it seemed. There was no reason to hate each other for that. But there was also no reason to try to make things work when we were so different.

Parking the truck, I wondered how she'd take me coming into the bar. It had been a whole month. It took a fair amount of courage to get my feet to take me inside, but they finally did. I saw Joey behind the bar. "Is Bobbi Jo around?" I held up the bag with Dairy King written on the side of it. "I've got a delivery to make."

"Since when did you start working at the Dairy King, Cash?" he asked with a smile.

"A few minutes ago." I saw Bobbi Jo's little blonde head coming out of the back. When she looked up at me, our eyes locked. "Hey."

She looked off to one side quickly. "Hey."

I put the bag on the bar. "I brought your order."

"Thanks." She walked behind the bar, then grabbed the bag, putting it underneath it.

"You're not hungry?" I asked. "Oh, and I paid off your tab, too."

Her eyes flashed at me, then away. "You didn't need to do that."

"Well, I did it anyway." I drummed my fingers on the bar. "So, how about a beer?"

Joey poured me one. "Have a seat. Stay a while." He put the frosted mug full of beer in front of me.

"That okay with you, Bobbi Jo?"

"Sure." She didn't look at me as she began dusting off bottles on the shelves.

I took a seat, then thought about what I could say to make her stop being so uptight. Although I'd had no intentions at all of talking about the skating rink, I had nothing else to talk about, so it popped out. "I think I've found the perfect spot for that thing we talked about."

She stopped dusting to turn and look at me. "The rink?"

I nodded. "Yeah."

She smiled. "That empty lot not too far away from the Dairy King?"

Nodding again, I asked, "You think the same thing?"

"I have." The way she smiled made my heart pound in my chest. But I had to remember what Tiffany had told me. Sex wasn't a thing I was supposed to be thinking about. "Are you still thinking about doing that?"

"Kind of." I had thought a lot about it. The thing was, it was something she and I were going to do together. Without her, there didn't seem to be any reason to get serious about it.

"Well, that would be a prime spot." She pulled out the food I'd brought her and began to get it out of the bag, her appetite back, it seemed.

I chewed on my lower lip as I thought about what to say next. "Maybe we could have a little snack bar there too. You know, corn-chip pies, corn dogs, lobster rolls. You remember those lobster rolls we had? They might be a real big seller here."

"They sure might." She took a bite of her burger. "But it would be a lot of work to get that all going. Do you think you've got that kind of time?"

"I've got nothing but time."

"Yeah, I'm sure you do." She took a sip of her soda. "I think you'll do a great job of it, Cash. I really do."

"Well, I can't do it alone." I hoped I wasn't pushing it too fast.

"I would assume it would be best to get some help." She took a bite of the pickle that had come with it.

"How about you?" I asked then held my breath for her answer.

"Me?" She shook her head and my heart stopped beating. "Not me, Cash. We don't think along the same lines. You'll find someone who thinks like you do. I'm sure you will. And I wish you all the luck in the world with that project. I think I can even make up a recipe for those lobster rolls. I can still taste them sometimes."

"Well, I've got to include you somehow, Bobbi Jo. You were the one who came up with that whole idea." I wasn't about to leave her out of anything.

"Nah." She took another bite of her burger, then walked away as if that was all she needed to say.

But there was a hell of a lot more left to say, and I wasn't about to take no for an answer.

CHAPTER TWENTY

Bobbi Jo

I thought it was pretty weird how Cash decided to come in that very day. And with the talk of the skating rink too? Well, it was all a bit too weird.

Cash mentioning the business we'd talked a little about before our breakup—which hadn't been so much a breakup since we hadn't been serious—really threw me. "I can't spread myself out that thin, Cash. I've got my own things going now."

"What kind of things do you have going on now?" he asked as if he didn't believe me.

Joey answered that for me. "Bobbi Jo was gifted this bar on Friday. She's now the new owner of The Watering Hole."

The way Cash sat there, his mouth hanging open, made me laugh. "That surprises you?"

"Well, yeah." He took a drink of his beer. "How did that happen?"

I looked at Joey who went to check on the tables and refill drinks as I went back to the bar, leaning on it. "Mr. and Mrs. Langford have owned the bar for years. They moved to Abilene when I first started working here. I've been managing it for them all these years. Mr.

Langford passed away a couple of weeks ago. Mrs. Langford is going to live in Montana with her oldest daughter. She didn't want the trouble of the bar anymore, so she gifted it to me. And along with that, she gave me the sum of fifty-thousand dollars to make it my own. You know, fix it up the way I want it? I've been thinking about what I would like to do to make this place feel like mine."

"I don't know what to say." He looked around the place. "It needs a lot of work, doesn't it?"

"Oh, I don't know." I looked around too. "The locals don't seem to have a problem with it."

"Yeah, but most of them haven't seen much outside of town." He smiled suddenly. "Why not let me be your partner, Bobbi Jo?"

"Um." I didn't know what to say. "I don't know. We think so differently."

He rolled his eyes. "No, we don't. I was wrong, Bobbi Jo. I don't know what I was thinking. I don't know why I wanted to go to New York when we hadn't even talked about what we both liked yet. I rushed it."

"Like you're trying to rush me into partnering with you now?" I wasn't about to rush into anything—especially now.

He took a deep breath then let it out slowly. "I don't know why I'm this way with you—it kind of drives me crazy. Look, I've missed you. And I'm supposed to be saying all sorts of other things, but the main thing is that I have missed you, Bobbi Jo. I miss your smile, your laugh, that dimple on your left ass cheek. I miss it all."

"I would be lying if I said that I haven't missed you, Cash. But things are different. I've got this bar to run now. And some other things have come up too. I'm going to be busy, quite frankly." I didn't know what else to say to the man. "It was fun. It really was. But life is getting busy for me. I can't run off anymore. I can't spend my nights not getting any rest."

"I haven't asked you to do that." He got up and walked away, looking kind of upset, then came right back and sat down. "Look, I want more. Okay, there it is. I want you. I want to do this right this time. I was only fooling myself before. I'm done playing. So, what do you say?"

"What are you asking?" I knew what he was asking, but I wanted him to say it—actually say the words.

"You know what I want." He looked at me with soft eyes. "You know what I'm asking."

I couldn't help but smile. "That means a lot, Cash. I know how hard that was for you to not say." Laughing, I knew he wasn't ready for the real deal. "I've got more to consider now. Playing at love isn't enough for me."

"I'm sorry?" Cash wore a frown. "Playing at love?"

"You don't love me," I stated. "And I don't love you."

"But we do care about each other." He wasn't about to just let things end there. "Love will come. I know it will."

"It could." I shrugged. "But now I'm just not into it. You know what I'm saying? I've got so much to think about now." And I really did have so much to think about. I had no idea how I could possibly fit Cash into my life now.

"Besides this bar, what else do you have going on that would stop you from seeing me?"

But I wasn't going to be spreading news until I was sure there was news to spread. "It's not a good time for me to be getting involved in a romantic relationship. And as far as the business relationship you've expressed interest in, that's out for now too. I want to do *me*, Cash. Can't you understand that?"

"No," came his stoic answer. "I can't see you wanting to just do you, Bobbi Jo. There is no reason to. If you don't want me in your business, then I can respect that. If you don't want me in your bed, I've got to know why that is. Is someone else in it?"

"This town is too small for me to hide a man from you, Cash. I think you know that." I didn't even want another man. "If things weren't so weird right now, I might've taken you up on your generous offer of having a relationship. That is what you've offered, right?"

He nodded. "But if I can be honest, I'm beginning to wish I hadn't even brought it up. I'm kind of feeling a little naked and vulnerable here."

"I bet you are." Boy, I knew that feeling.

"And you're not making it any better." He looked at me as if only I could help him out.

"Look, Cash. I don't know what to do for you. To me, you made the decision that you didn't want to hang with me anymore after our trip to New York." I understood that he liked stuff and I didn't. I didn't think it meant we couldn't still see each other, but apparently he did. "So, why do you want me now? I still hate New York."

"Well, I just realized that I hate it too." He threw his hands up in the air. "There it is. I hated the same things you did. But the difference between me and you is, I gave it a chance before deciding I hated it."

"And I knew I hated it right off the bat." I smiled at him. "What I gave a chance was you. I gave you the chance to see if you liked me or not. And you didn't call or come by to see me, letting me know you didn't like me. I guessed you didn't like me being so honest with you. No matter what it was, you didn't want to talk to me or see me anymore. And guess what, I got over it, Cash."

"No, you did not." He shook his head. "You're not over me."

"I think I am." I picked up a towel to wipe the bar down. "I really do. It hurt that first week when I kept waiting for that call or for you to come in here to see me. But that second week, it got a little easier. The third week, well, I was over it by then."

"The hell you were." He drank down the rest of the beer. "Stop playing. I know I was wrong. I know I was trying to be something I wasn't, and you were just being you. I was wrong, okay? Are you going to make me beg you to come back to me?"

"Most certainly not." I rubbed the bar down as I tried not to get myself in a tizzy over what he was saying.

Did I yearn to feel Cash's strong arms around me again? Sure.

Did I still fall asleep thinking about the man? Well, yes, of course I did.

But was I about to let him back into my heart when he could so easily shut me out? No way in hell.

"It seems like you want me to beg." He looked me in the eyes. "I will beg if that's what you really want."

"Please don't." I didn't want to see him beg. "Really, Cash. You walked away from me for me just being who I am. We never really got to know one another. We got into having sex too soon. It happens. We like the sex we had, and we would like to have more of it. But I can't. Not anymore."

"I do like you."

I shook my head. "No, you don't. I wish I would've taken a picture of your face when I told you I didn't like that hotel. You are exactly the kind of man I guessed you were. You are a rich man who wants the kinds of things rich men want. And I am a woman who is down to earth. I want modest things—simple things. Go get what you want and let me have this little chunk of Heaven I've always had in Carthage."

"So you never want to travel?" he asked me.

"I didn't say that." I did have interest in other places. "There are lots of places I'd love to see and things I'd love to experience. And one day, if we ever get to really know one another, you will find out where those places are."

He tapped the bar. "I don't want you to tell me. I want to figure it out myself. You think I don't know you, but I do. I do know you, Bobbi Jo Baker. You'll see."

"I wouldn't bother if I were you." I put the towel away as I smiled at him. "I really do have my hands too full now to put my heart at risk any longer."

"Your heart?" he asked. "I thought you didn't want to get serious either. I thought you didn't want a boyfriend."

"I didn't. I don't." I had more than I could handle now. Cash would only be in my way. "I had a good time with you for the most part. Let's not ruin it."

"I already have." He looked down. "I don't know why I quit talking to you. I really don't. I was being stupid. Maybe I wanted to be something I wasn't. Maybe I was using you as an excuse. I don't know. All I know is that life isn't fun without you in it." He looked up at me. "Is your life fun without me in it?"

I couldn't lie. "You made it a lot more fun, Cash."

"And you don't want that fun back?"

I did, but then again, I knew I couldn't have things the way they had been. I was pretty damn sure Cash wouldn't be happy with the way I would have to live now. "Cash, it was fun. And now things have to change. I'm not saying fun is completely out, but it's got to take a back burner as life gets going for me."

"What does that even mean, Bobbi Jo?"

In time, he would find out, but for now, I wasn't ready to elaborate on it.

CHAPTER TWENTY-ONE

Cash

I'd left the bar confused, a little aggravated, and even a bit hurt. I knew it was all my fault, all my doing, and it was all up to me to put things back together again. But now, Bobbi Jo seemed to be over me —like totally over me. That didn't sit well with me—not even a little bit.

Jasper and Tyrell were in the barn when I drove up. All the outside lights were on, and that meant something was going down. I walked into the barn to find pretty much everyone who lived on the ranch hanging out inside. With a cow on the ground, I pretty much knew why the gathering was going on. "She about to have a calf?"

My brothers nodded.

"Yep," Tyrell said. "She's the oldest cow we've got. We're all pretty interested in how well she does."

The things people on a ranch were interested in boggled my mind at times. Like the day we found a rouge weed in the hayfield. Detailed analysis had to be done to figure out how that weed had even gotten into that hayfield. I swear, I thought the ranch foreman had been about to call in the FBI over that dang weed. And now we had an old cow giving birth. The possibilities of entertainment never seemed to end.

I leaned up against the wall, careful to avoid looking directly at the expectant mother. Staring at them while in labor tended to piss them off. "So, I talked to Bobbi Jo a little while ago."

Jasper made a weird sound. "Finally. Did she give you the time of day after you blew her off the way you did? Because I had my bets that she wouldn't say two words to you, little bro."

"She talked to me." I gave him the stink eye. "I didn't do anything so mean to her to warrant her not speaking to me at all."

Tyrell coughed as if that was ridiculous. "Um, giving her the cold shoulder for a month ain't exactly being nice, Cash."

I knew that. "I meant I didn't talk ugly to her. I didn't talk behind her back. I didn't start seeing anyone else. Other than not talking to her, I didn't do anything wrong. And I wanted to get together with her in a real way this time."

"Did you ask her to get back together with you?" Jasper asked.

"Yeah." I kicked the dirt floor.

"And she must've turned you down," Tyrell said.

I nodded. "And not just for the relationship either. She turned me down as a business partner too."

Jasper laughed quietly so as not to disturb the laboring cow. "Can you blame her? You don't have five minutes of experience running a business, Cash."

"So?" I didn't know what else to say, then thought of something important. "But I do have money and lots of it. I could be a great business partner. Anyone would want me."

"Yeah," Tyrell agreed. "To use your money. What kind of business did you entice Bobbi Jo with anyway?"

"Well, at first it was this old-fashioned skating rink that we'd talked about when we took our trip. But then I found out that she's now the new owner of the bar and I offered to help her out with that." I shoved my hands into my pockets, fisting them with aggravation. "But she politely refused my help. She kept saying how she didn't have time for fun and life had to move on and dumb shit like that."

Jasper and Tyrell looked at each other as Jasper said, "A skating rink sounds fun, doesn't it?"

Tyrell nodded. "Yeah, it does. Maybe we should make one out here."

I had to interject. "No, not out here. In town, where everyone can go and enjoy it."

Tyrell smiled at me. "Yeah, in town. That's a great idea. We should do that. All three of us. We could call it the Whisper Roller Skating Rink. I like it."

Jasper added, "We could use our ranch's brand as the logo. That would be great."

"I had this idea about having a little snack bar in there too," I told them. "Bobbi Jo and I had these killer lobster rolls while we were in Maine. They were served as appetizers at the place we ate at. They were mini hotdog buns filled with lobster that was made a lot like tuna fish salad. But you could make full-size versions of them too."

"A snack bar?" Jasper asked. "That might step on Dairy King's toes a bit, don't ya think?"

"How could it?" I asked. "If we don't sell anything they do, then how could it hurt their business?"

Tyrell shook his head. "The only place I can think of in town where a rink that size could fit is that empty lot not even two blocks away from the Dairy King. If we served any food at all, it would take away from their business. And I ain't about to do that to Tiffany's family."

Jasper agreed. "Yeah, me neither. So, we can have a rink but no snack bar."

"Well, fine." But I didn't even want to do a business with my brothers in the first place. "Then that's your guy's thing. I'll just think of something else." But all I could think of involved Bobbi Jo. But she didn't want to have a business with me either.

I kicked the dirt again, and Jasper put his hand on my shoulder. "Send her some flowers, little bro."

Tyrell came around to stand on the other side of me, putting his hand on my other shoulder. "Send her some chocolates too. Girls love chocolates."

Jasper asked, "Did you tell her how sorry you were?"

Tyrell added, "Did you tell her how stupid you were?"

Jasper went on, "Did you tell her that you were wrong?"

Tyrell had to add one more thing. "Did you tell her how lucky you were to ever have her in the first place?"

"I did apologize. I did tell her that I was wrong. But I didn't tell her how lucky I was." Maybe that would've been the one thing that would've worked. "I'm going to follow your advice, brothers. Operation flowers and candy will begin in the morning. And after that, I'll let her know—without a doubt—that she was the best thing to ever happen to me."

Jasper cocked one brow at me as he asked, "Cash, when did this begin to set into your brain? I mean, yesterday you were still sullen about her and how she acted on that trip. What made today any different than the past month?"

I needed to be honest. "I had this dream early this morning, just before I woke up. It was the first dream I've ever had about Bobbi Jo. She wasn't exactly there, but her voice was. She kept calling out to me, and I kept going toward her voice, but I never could find her."

"Surreal," Jasper said. "A disembodied voice calling to you, using Bobbi Jo's southern twang."

I punched him in the arm. "Come on. You asked me when this came to me, and it was this morning, and that was why. No reason to make fun of me."

Tyrell looked at Jasper with a stern expression. "Yeah, don't make fun of the little dreamer." He patted me on the back. "But I think that dream was a little too faint to be the actual reason you sought her out this evening. You had to have been thinking about her before that."

I got quiet as I knew it was time to admit something. "I've never stopped thinking about her."

Jasper smacked me on the back. "See! Now, that makes more sense. So why did you stop yourself from going to see her or even talking to her in this last month?"

"It was the trip. It was the way she acted on it. She was so comfortable with telling me how she didn't like things." I looked at the ground, trying to make sense out of how that had made me feel.

"Don't you want her to feel comfortable with you, Cash?" Tyrell asked.

"I thought I did, but then I didn't." I looked at him. "Because no girl has ever been that comfortable with me. And to be honest, it makes me feel like she doesn't even like me that much if she's that damn comfortable with me."

Jasper's eyes went big. "Are you shitting me?"

I shook my head. "No." All the girls I've ever had anything to do with walked on eggshells around me. Like they were afraid to show who they really were for fear I'd stop seeing them."

"And then one of them finally *did* show you who she really was and you ghosted her," Tyrell pointed out. "Weird, huh?"

"I think it's time to stop being so immature, Cash," Jasper told me. "Bobbi Jo should be able to be who she is without fear of you dumping her."

It came crashing in on me all at once. Bobbi Jo was a strong, secure woman. She got one whiff of my immaturity and knew she didn't like that one bit. No wonder she didn't seem to be mad at me. She just didn't think that much of me anymore.

"Wow, I'm an ass. I have never wanted to think of myself in that fashion, but that's exactly what I've been all these years. And Bobbi Jo is just woman enough not to want to deal with that crap." I looked at the cow as it let out a loud huffing sound.

Her big brown eyes met mine, and she seemed to be looking right into my soul. For what seemed like forever, that cow and I looked into each other's eyes then she closed hers as the ranch foreman shouted, "We've got a girl!"

"Way to go," I whispered to the cow. "You didn't let age get in your way, did ya, old girl?"

I was the baby of the family—the youngest Gentry brother. Maybe I hadn't thought about growing up much. No, scratch that. I had never thought about growing up.

Somewhere deep inside of me, I liked the fact that women didn't feel comfortable enough with me to be themselves around me. I liked the fact they pretended to like things I did, just to please me. I had been a shallow fool.

I didn't even want to be that kind of guy anymore. I wanted to grow the hell up. I wanted to start maturing. But how?

"Tyrell, how can I stop being so damn immature?"

"Thinking about other people is a start," he told me. "Letting people be who they are, without fear of you judging them or not wanting anything to do with them is also a good idea. Going to Bobbi Jo and admitting everything is also something a mature man would do."

"Maybe you're right." I didn't know if just admitting that I'd been wrong and immature would be enough for Bobbi Jo. She really didn't seem to want me anymore. "Well, I'm going to hit the hay since she's had her baby."

Leaving the barn, I walked through the dark, starry night and wondered why I'd been the way I'd been all my life. Not realizing that you'd been immature was a real drag. Like what else had I not realized about myself through the years?

As I walked up to my room, I took each step slowly. I wasn't in a rush to get into my bed alone that night. Everything felt empty. For the first time in my life, I felt empty.

This feels like crap.

CHAPTER TWENTY-TWO

Bobbi Jo

The sound of the doorbell ringing woke me up from a deep and restful sleep. I heard Betty Sue shout, "I'll get it. I saw flowers coming up the sidewalk. I'm sure it's for me."

I snuggled back down, sure they were for her too. But then a few minutes later, the bedroom door opened and in came a mountain of flowers. "Surprise, Bobbi Jo. These are for you."

Rubbing my eyes, I sat up. "Huh?"

Betty Sue put the vase full of all kinds of flowers on my desk. "These are for you, Bobbi Jo." She took the card out of them and handed it to me. "I know who they're from. I don't even have to read the card to know that."

The envelope was much bigger than the normal ones that come with flowers. "What is this man doing?" I opened the envelope and out spilled a gift card to Amazon and a thank you card.

"Read it out loud, Bobbi Jo," Betty Sue urged me.

"Okay." I opened the card. "I just wanted to thank you, Bobbi Jo. You gave me more than I could have ever hoped for. I had the chance to see things through your eyes, and I blew it. I know that now. You were right. That bed was hard as a rock. And the city did have a smell to it too. You were right about everything, and I am man enough to admit when he's been wrong. Thanks for opening my eyes to the immature, little jackass I've been my whole life. Sincerely, Cash."

I put the card down to look at the flowers as I noticed Betty Sue's gaping mouth. "Wow. I don't think I've ever had a man say or write anything like that to me before. And I've had quite a few immature jackasses in my time."

"It's not like I even care." I put the card down, making sure to put the gift card in it. "I don't hate Cash. Not even a little. I just have better things to do with my time now." I ran my hand over my still flat stomach.

Betty Sue looked over the massive amount of flowers. "He had to have ordered these online. The delivery driver wasn't from around here. I've never seen these types of flowers in Miss Loretta's shop downtown either."

"What are you still doing home?" I asked, as she should've been at work a long time ago.

"I've been feeling a little under the weather lately. I don't know why but I keep having the dry heaves. It's so weird." She put her hand on her stomach. "My tummy's all wiggly inside sometimes, and then I feel like I'm going to puke. It's so weird. I asked the nurse at work what it might be and she said I might be getting lactose intolerant. So, I cut out drinking milk. But so far that hasn't helped much at all."

Not always, but at times, my twin and I could feel things the other felt. There was this one week back when we first started high school where Betty Sue was having nightmares, and then I began getting them too. And they were identical as well. It was weird, and then it went away.

And I once broke my pinky finger when a friend accidentally slammed it in a car door. Betty Sue had felt that and had actually come home from summer camp, where she'd been. She wanted to go to the hospital, sure she had cancer since there was no reason for her finger to hurt so badly. Our parents were stunned when they found out I'd broken my finger. And the thing that had been even crazier was that as soon as Betty Sue found out what had happened to me, her finger stopped hurting.

I wondered if her illness would stop if I told her why *I* felt sick. But I wasn't sure about telling anyone just yet. It was so early on, and anything could happen. If things didn't go the way I thought they would, I didn't want a lot of sympathy.

Getting out of bed, I figured I might as well get up. I was thinking about the bar and how I had to make some pretty drastic changes there. And I had a move to think about too. "I should get up. There's lots to be done now."

"With your new ownership of the bar?" she asked.

Nodding, I went to pick out some clothes. "I want to put an ad in the paper for another bartender. I'd like to take a few steps back if I can. Maybe not stay up late anymore. You know, sit back and let others do the hard work while I rake in the dough?"

"That would be smart." Betty Sue put her hand back on her stomach. "Ugh. Maybe I have a bug. It just hits me, then it's gone. It's so weird."

"That is weird," I said. "Anyway, I've gotta get ready to face the day. The sooner I get someone hired, the sooner I can get to doing the real work with the bar. I'm thinking about adding in a grill. That will mean hiring a cook and some prep staff too. And maybe even a waitress or runners or something like that. I want the place to start bringing in more customers, and I want them to spend more of their money at the bar. I'm going to take some online business courses too. I want to make the most out of this opportunity."

"Good." Betty Sue sat on her bed. "Maybe you can finally move out and I can have this room to myself."

With a smile, I nodded. "That is one of my plans. But there's a lot to do first." Time was limited though, so I knew I had to get my butt moving.

After a shower, I got dressed, then headed out. Going to the office where the local newspaper was published, I put an ad in the paper for a bartender. Then I went to the health department to get all the information I would need to put a kitchen into the bar.

Hours later, the need to eat crept up on me just after I'd finished with the health department. I was close to the Dairy King, so I walked over to grab a bite.

Just as I walked in, I saw Cash sitting in a booth. His eyes met mine. I nodded, made my order, then went to say hello and thank him for the flowers. I stood at the end of his table. "Hi. I got the flowers, the card, and the gift card. It was all very nice of you."

"Do you accept my sincere apology?" he asked.

I did accept it. "Cash, it's okay. You are who you are. I know you want someone around who wants to do what you do. And most girls will be more than happy to go along with whatever you want. Just not me."

"Would you like to sit down?" he asked me as he nodded at the empty seat across from him. "I'd like to talk if that's okay with you?"

I had some time to spare. "Okay." I sat.

"My brothers want to make that skating rink." He paused as if waiting for me to say something about that.

"Cool."

He nodded. "Okay. I wasn't sure if you would be mad about that or not."

"Why would I be mad?" He really didn't understand me. "It's a great idea, and if they want to do it, that's great. I don't have the money to make that happen anyway."

"Okay," he said, seeming a little off. "One of the cows had a calf last night when I got home. She was looking at me when she had it. It was weird."

"I bet it was." I smiled at the girl who brought me my order. "Thanks, Bethy."

"You're welcome." She turned to walk away.

But I stopped her. "Hey, Bethy, I'd like to ask you a question if you don't mind."

She stopped and came back. "Sure. What is it?"

"I'm thinking about adding a grill to the bar. Do you think I would need waitresses and do traditional service? Or would an order station and runners make more sense?"

"Def an order station and runners. It's so much easier." Bethy smiled. "And I'd love to work for you, Bobbi Jo. I bet the tips would be great."

"Me too." I gave her a smile. "When I get it going, you'll be on the list of runners for sure. And if there's anyone you know who can work as a bartender, it would be great if you sent them my way. I'm going to stop working nights as soon as I can."

"I'll let you know." She left, and when I looked back at Cash, I found him grinning.

"You're not going to be working nights anymore?"

"Not after I get another bartender. I've got better things to do with my time. Or I will have." I took a drink of my water, then dug into my salad."

His eyes went to the food in front of me. "Salad?"

Nodding, I said, "I'm watching what I eat. It's not about my weight; it's about nutrition. I want to take in only highly nutritious foods and drinks."

He nodded. "Okay. And about the bar. If you're not going to be tending the bar, what are you going to be doing?"

"Just running it." I took another bite as he looked out the window, seeming lost in thought.

"From home or what?" he asked. "There's no office in the bar itself."

"Not yet, there's not." I was still unsure of where I'd make my office. "But I don't know for sure if I'll make one down there or maybe at my place. I'm going to move out of my parents' house."

"And when is that going to happen?" He took a sip of his coke as he looked at me.

"Whenever I find a place that suits me." I wanted something nice. "At least two bedrooms, but it would be best if it had three. I could use one for my office that way."

"And you would use the other bedroom for what?" he asked.

His question pulled me out of my head for a moment. "Huh?"

He smiled. "You said you wanted a three bedroom. One room for you. One room for your office. And one room for what else?"

"Oh," I said as I tried not to seem as if I was making a big deal about it. "You know if something ever came up. You know what I'm saying."

"Nope." He eyed me. "You're looking very pretty today, Bobbi Jo. You have this glow about you." His hands moved over the table toward mine. "I truly am sorry for how I've acted. And I know you might not think that I can change, but I'd like the opportunity to prove it to you."

The sound of my cell buzzing in my pocket had me pulling my hands away from his. "I need to check this. I've got an ad out in the paper about the bartender. It might be about that." When I looked at the text that had come in, I saw it was from my sister.

My chest filled with air as I took in a deep breath, then held it. She'd done some digging after I'd left the house, it seemed.

She knows.

CHAPTER TWENTY-THREE

Cash

"Shit," Bobbi Jo hissed. "Well, it looks like I need to go." She looked over her shoulder. "Bethy, can I get a box for this salad? I need to take it to go."

I saw no reason to hurry away. "What's the rush, Bobbi Jo? What's so important that it can't wait for you to finish eating your salad?"

"I've gotta get down to my dad's office before someone else does." She got up, boxed her salad, then hauled ass out the door.

Her bottle of water still sat on the table, and I stared at it. "What the hell?"

Nothing made sense to me, and I figured nothing would until I got Bobbi Jo to trust me again. I left the Dairy King.

The truck had to stay back at the ranch to get the oil changed by the mechanic, so I'd driven one of the Mercedes to town to grab some lunch. Chef Todd had made a shrimp dish for lunch. I hadn't been able to eat seafood since our trip. It just reminded too much of Bobbi Jo, and I hadn't wanted to be reminded of her. But now, I didn't want to stop thinking about her and how I had to fix things between us.

Just as I got into the car, I heard the sound of sirens filling the air.

I had to wait before pulling out as a white car with flashing red and blue lights sped by. That had been the source of all the noise. With it gone, the town went quiet again.

I pulled out, heading home. There wasn't anything else to do in town. I drove around the small town, looking at everything.

The town square was really nice, quaint, and something to be proud of. Small churches dotted the town too. I'd never taken the time to look at the town that would be my new home. It was not only nice, but hospitable, and pretty, too.

Calling Carthage home would be something I might come to even cherish someday. Bobbi Jo had lived her whole life in this place. I could see why she wanted to make her life here, do something here.

World traveling sounded great, but not nearly as great as making Carthage the place we'd live in the rest of our lives. My brothers had different ideas about what to do in the town to make it theirs. Bobbi Jo was going to fix up that bar to make it a place she could be proud to call her own. And what did I have?

Nothing.

I had nothing to call my own. Nothing to leave in this town that would tell future generations that Cash Gentry had once lived in Carthage, Texas.

There had to be something I could give this town. Something that no one else had ever given it.

My cell rang, and I tried to grab it from its place on the passenger seat. But I accidentally stepped on the brake a little too hard and sent it flying off the seat to the floor. When I hit the gas, I accelerated a little too hard and sent the phone sliding underneath the seat. "Well, crap." The pedals proved to be touchy in the beast of a machine.

My cell rang a few times, then went silent. I sighed then took the turn to head out to the ranch. Once I got there, I would fish it out and see whose call I'd missed.

The only person I really wanted to hear from probably wouldn't be the one calling me anyway. Bobbi Jo seemed to be perfectly all right without me. She looked happy even.

It began to sink in that she hadn't really liked me all that much in the first place. Maybe it had been all sex and nothing concrete at all. Maybe she saw through my shiny outer shell to my shallow insides. Maybe she hadn't liked what she'd found.

And who could blame her?

I had to be the richest loser in the world. No one could come close to being as bad as I was.

It might be the best thing for Bobbi Jo if I just left her alone and stopped trying. She deserved better than me. And now that she'd knocked some sense into her evil twin sister, that girl wouldn't get in the middle of Bobbi Jo and whatever new guy she found.

My gut twisted as I thought of my Bobbi Jo being with another man. But I didn't have the right to feel pain over that. *I'd* blown it. I'd had my chance and I'd thrown it away.

And all over the fact that she was just being honest and didn't like where I'd taken her. "Man, if I would've just taken her to Montana to eat steaks, this whole thing could've been avoided."

People in Texas were set in their ways; I had known that. We never ate Mexican food any further north than Austin. Anything after the Austin city limits sign wasn't authentic.

I'd made the mistake of choosing seafood for our first trip together. If she ever gave me the chance, I would never make the same mistakes again. But I highly doubted she'd ever give me another chance. Why would she?

I'd blown it—big time.

My cell went off again and one more time after that. I was beginning to think there was something pretty damn important someone wanted to tell me.

I heard a few text messages come in too. "Man, what the hell is up?"

In just a couple of minutes, I would be able to get the cell out from under the seat. I'd just turned into the ranch and was heading up the driveway. What I saw up ahead confused me.

Blue and red lights flashed in the afternoon sunlight. The white car that I'd seen in town was parked near the front entrance. And there was a tall man, his hand on his holster, his sunglass-covered eyes directed at me.

Tyrell stood at the door, his eyes on me too. He shook his head and moved his arms as if he wanted me to turn around and leave. And that was when a couple of gunshots were fired; the bullets zipped over the top of the car. I hit the accelerator by accident, as that had totally surprised me. "Fuck!"

Barreling toward the man who'd shot at me, I turned the wheel to miss him and hit the back end of his car. Airbags exploded around me, the sound of metal on metal met my ringing ears, then the car door came open. "You rat bastard! Get the fuck out of the car and put your hands where I can see 'em."

"What did I do?" I felt dizzy from the blow of the airbag. "What's going on?"

A hand came in, then I heard the sound of fabric being sliced with a knife. "Take that seatbelt off and get out!"

"Okay, okay," I muttered as I tried to make my hands work. "I'm kind of freaked out here, man."

"*You're* freaked out?" he hollered. "What about me? What do you think I am?"

"I don't know what or even *who* you are." I hit the button to release the seatbelt, then felt a hand on the back of my neck, jerking me out of the car.

Tyrell shouted, "Hey, you don't know if he's hurt or not! Don't go yanking on him like that!"

"Boy, you better shut up and let me deal with this piece of shit!" the man shouted back at my brother.

"Piece of shit?" I'd been called names a time or two in my life, but a piece of shit hadn't been one of them.

Suddenly, I was pushed to face the wrecked car; my head smacked against the top of the door. That was when my other brother showed up. I heard Jasper shout, "Oh, hell no!"

"You stay out of this!" the man who was roughing me up shouted back.

"You've got one second to get your hands off our little brother or, so help me God, you will never see the light of day again, old man!" Jasper yelled. "Do you know who you're messing with? We're the Gentry boys. We've got more money than God right now. And you won't have a pot to piss in if you don't get your hands off our brother!"

"Who are you?" I asked. "You've got the wrong man. I haven't broken even one law that I can remember in recent history."

"Boy, just shut up and listen to me." The man yanked me back then turned me to face him. "You and I need to talk—man to man. Call your brothers off and we'll settle this shit between us and us alone."

"I'm sorry about this, man, but I ain't about to tell my brothers to stay out of this." I wasn't some idiot. "I have no idea what's going on here. I don't know why you're pissed at me. But I do know that they will kick your ass and sue the shit out of you if you don't let me go."

He looked at his now beat up car and the sigh he let out told me he had no idea what he was going to do next. I had the impression he'd been planning on throwing me into that car and taking me away with him somewhere. "Fuck!"

"Yeah, it's a fucking shame you won't be able to kidnap me." I began to wonder if he'd planned to kidnap me and get ransom from my brothers. I asked him as much.

"What?" He shook his head then finally let go of me. "No. I ain't no kidnapper, you idiot. I was going to take you in. I was going to keep you in a cell while I got answers. I was going to make sure you couldn't run away from me and your responsibilities."

I had no idea what he was talking about. And then I heard my cell going off again. "Look, I need to get that phone and answer it. I'm afraid it might be important. It's been ringing like crazy for a while now."

"Not yet." He put the gun up to my side, the end of it stabbing a spot between my ribs. "If you do so much as try to move, I will put a bullet right in your heart. I can do it. Don't tempt me."

"I don't doubt that you can do it," I told him. "But I would love to know why you *would* do it. Sir," I threw that last part in to try to deescalate the rather dangerous situation.

Tyrell and Jasper moved in, flanking the man on either side as Tyrell said, "Look, mister, we've called the police. You had better let our brother go or there will be hell to pay."

Our driveway was a mile long and already the squeals of tires could be heard as cars turned on it, coming to my rescue. "Come on, man," I said. "We don't have to do this. We can talk. Something is obviously bothering you."

"Put the gun down," Tyrell said. "Come on, now. Things don't have to go like this."

Jasper added, "We don't want anyone to get hurt."

The sound of tires crunching gravel met my ears. Then the tires slid to a stop, followed by the creak of a car door. "Daddy, no!"

I glanced in the direction of the familiar voice. "Bobbi Jo?"

CHAPTER TWENTY-FOUR

Bobbi Jo

I'd never felt more embarrassed. But seeing my daddy with his gun in Cash's ribcage proved to be the most embarrassed I'd ever been. "Daddy, no!"

Cash looked at me out of the corner of his eye. "Bobbi Jo?" He looked at my dad. "This is your father?"

"Yes." I got up next to my father, putting my hand on top of his, pulling the gun back away from Cash. "Daddy, stop. You've got to stop. We need to go. You shouldn't even be here."

I managed to get my father to back up with me as a couple of his deputies pulled up and got out to see what the ruckus was all about. He held up his gun then put it in his holster. "It's okay, boys. You all can go back to the station. I'm calm now."

"You sure you don't want them to stay?" Cash asked. "It might be better if they stayed."

"It's okay, Cash. Daddy won't hurt you," I let him know. "He was just upset." I looked at my father's car that had a Mercedes up its ass. "Wow, what happened here?"

"I hit the car." Cash shrugged. "I wasn't used to the pedals and hit the accelerator instead of the brake. In my defense though, he was shooting at me when I did it."

I couldn't believe my father had done that. "Daddy!"

"Well, he was going to try to make a run for it," he said.

"Was not," Cash retaliated. "There was no reason to try to run. Well, until you went and fired a gun at me, there wasn't."

Jasper cleared his throat. "Maybe we should all go inside and get to the bottom of this."

I didn't want to get to the bottom of anything. "No. That's okay. I'll just take my father and leave you boys alone."

Cash put his hand on my arm to stop me. "No. We need to find out what has your father so upset with me, Bobbi Jo. I would rather not have this happen again."

"Yeah? Well, it won't." I looked at my father who now seemed a lot more settled.

Tyrell wasn't about to let it go either. "No, we're going to get to the bottom of this, Bobbi Jo. We can't just allow things like this to happen."

My father growled. "Just let me deal with him."

"No." I took a deep breath then just came out with it. "Look, my father is worried about some things that he really doesn't need to be worried about. That's all. That's it. So, I'll straighten this out, and we'll get out of your hair." I looked at my father's car. "Do you think your car is drivable, Dad?"

"Not sure." He huffed. "Boy can't even drive right. What kind of a—"

I stopped him from saying what I knew he would say. "Anyway, let's get going. We can see if it'll start." I looked at Tyrell. "My apologies, Tyrell."

Jasper was the next one to stop me from leaving. "Wait a minute, Bobbi Jo. You're acting weird."

"She is," Cash agreed. "What's up, Bobbi Jo?"

"Just tell him," my father said. "Tell him so we can deal with this already."

Cash wouldn't let go of my arm. "Tell me, Bobbi Jo."

I had no intentions of telling anyone anything until things were more written in stone. "My stupid sister is what the problem is."

"I can't imagine what she could've done that would have all this happening," Cash said. "So fill us in."

"Betty Sue called me at work," my father said.

I hurried to add, "To tell him things that really were none of her business *nor* her concern."

Dad sighed then pulled his sunglasses off, looking at Cash. "Boy, you've done gone and got my daughter pregnant." He glared at me. "See, it's out there. Now, what are you gonna do about it?"

Cash stood there, perfectly still. He looked as if his mind was doing somersaults. "Huh?"

Before I could say anything, Dad said, "You're going to be a father, Cash Gentry." He looked at me again. "And I came here to find out what he's going to do about that."

"Well, Daddy, it's up to me what will happen with this baby. Now let's go." I tried to take a step away, but Cash hadn't let me go yet.

His grip on my arm only got tighter. "Wait a second, Bobbi Jo." He took a deep breath as his brothers got behind him.

"It's okay, Cash," Tyrell told him.

"You're going to be fine," Jasper added.

I found it kind of hard to believe they were all so worried about him and not so much about me. "Well, anyway, I am sure you will be fine, Cash. We'll get going now. Come on, Dad."

"Hold on." Cash pulled me to him, his eyes on mine. "Bobbi Jo? Are we having a baby?"

"*I* am having a baby." I had never expected anything out of him. "*Me*, Cash. *I* am having this baby."

My father wasn't about to shut up. "It's his responsibility too, Bobbi Jo. That's what I was trying to tell you, but you wouldn't listen to me."

Cash whispered, "I want it too, Bobbi Jo. It's my baby too."

My father sighed with relief. "Yes. Thank God. He wants it too. Hallelujah!"

"Can we talk about this later, Cash?" I really didn't want to discuss any of this with any of the people who were huddled around us.

"Why not hammer out the details now?" my father asked. "Cash, you up for that?"

"Sure," Cash said. "I'm up for that." He tugged me to go with him. "Let's all go inside and we can talk."

"I don't want to talk right now." I wasn't going to be forced into doing anything.

My father wasn't letting up though. "Cash, I don't know what's going on in my daughter's brain right now, but all I want to know is this: will you be marrying my daughter and doing what's right by her and this baby?"

I dropped my head, feeling heat course through my body as embarrassment overtook me. "Dad, no. We're not going to get—"

Cash interrupted me. "Marry me, Bobbi Jo Baker."

I could not believe what I'd heard him say. Slowly, I pulled my head up to look at him. "You don't mean that."

He nodded. "Yes, I do. Marry me."

My father let out a shout. "Yahoo! Yippee! There's gonna be a wedding! And here I was thinking that I would have to get out my gun again, boy!"

"No need, sir." Cash was all smiles. "I'll gladly marry your daughter."

With all the smiles and high fives going around, no one noticed that I hadn't exactly accepted Cash's proposal. "Um, excuse me. I haven't said yes."

Daddy laughed and picked me up, twirling me around like I was a little girl. "But you will, darlin', you will! Yahoo!"

Cash took me away from my father, planting a kiss on my lips. "We're going to be so happy, Bobbi Jo. I swear we will."

I could hardly speak as my father shouted. "Look at this place. My grandkid is going to live here. What a hell of a deal this kid has gotten, I tell you what."

Jasper put his hand on my shoulder as Cash refused to let me go.

"Congratulations, Bobbi Jo. Being a parent is the most rewarding experience in the history of experiences."

Tyrell nodded. "I'm so happy for you, Bobbi Jo."

"But I haven't said yes." No one seemed to hear me. I leaned in close to Cash's ear, hoping he'd listen to me. "Cash, I don't want to marry you."

"Huh?" Cash looked at me, the smile still on his face. "What did you say, baby?"

"I *don't* want to marry you." I put my hands against his chest to show him that I wanted to be let go. "Cash, I want to do this on my own. That's why I didn't rush to tell you. I want to do this my myself."

My father made a sound like a geyser had just blown up. "The hell you say, girl? You can't have a baby all on your own. First of all, it ain't just your baby. Tell her, Cash."

"Yeah, Cash, tell me." I stared him in the eyes, daring him to say the baby wasn't just mine.

It was my body that would carry this baby. Cash saw the look in my eyes. "I want to be here for you and the baby. Don't you want that?"

"I don't know what I want yet. But I know this: I will not be forced into a marriage. I will not be forced into a relationship with you, Cash Gentry. I don't care if you are the father; I will make the choices for this child."

My father huffed. "That's just stupid, Bobbi Jo. This man has lots of money."

"And I don't want any of it. I never have." I wasn't going to go down as the talk of the town. The barmaid who duped poor Cash Gentry into marrying her after getting herself pregnant just to get to his money.

"No one said you did, Bobbi Jo," Cash whispered. "Girl, I *want* to marry you. Do you understand what I am saying to you? I want this. I *want* you and I *want* our baby. And I know you didn't do this on purpose. I also know this a baby deserves both parents."

"This is *my* baby," I let him know. "Until I say any different, this baby is mine and mine alone. You don't know for sure that you're the father."

My father made a whooping sound. "Girl, if you weren't grown and pregnant right now, I would be whooping your hind-end right about now. Now, you know damn good and well that this man is the father of that baby. And I ain't about to let you go making him think anything else."

Cash let me go; he stepped back and looked me in the eyes. "Bobbi Jo, I don't want to make you do anything you don't want to do. I just want you to know that I am here for you and I want to do the right thing. But I will respect your wishes."

"Damn it, Bobbi Jo!" Dad yelled. "Now look at what you've gone and done. He wants to do the right thing. Let him."

I walked toward my car. "I'm leaving, Dad. Get a ride from one of your deputies if your car won't start." I got into my car and turned around, careful not to look at any of the faces that looked at me.

Not one of them knew how I felt. Not one of them knew what it would mean to me if I married a man who not only didn't love me but didn't even like me.

Cash was destined to marry someone else. Some woman was out there who wanted to dine on snails and eat goose liver. Some woman was out there who could find beauty in everything. Even things that stunk and had uncomfortable beds. I wasn't her. I wasn't Cash's dream woman.

My cell rang, and I saw my sister's number on it. So I answered her call. "You little betraying rat. I don't have a sister anymore."

Before I could hang up, she said, "I didn't do it for you or Cash. I did it for that baby. Think about that before you go disowning me, sister."

CHAPTER TWENTY-FIVE

Cash

After watching her drive away, I stumbled inside. I was going to be a father. Even if Bobbi Jo didn't want to share the kid with me, I was going to be a father.

Ella and Tiffany were talking softly in the next room as I came in to ask them some questions. "Um, I don't mean to interrupt you two, but I've got a question that I think only a woman would understand."

Tiffany smiled at me. "Sure, Cash. Ask Away."

"So, Bobbi Jo just told me she's pregnant, and when I asked her to marry me, she said no. And I'd just really like to understand why she said that." I rocked on my heels as I felt like I might collapse.

Both sets of eyes went wide, then Ella's hand went over her mouth as she squealed. "Wow! Congrats, Cash!"

Tiffany got up and came to hug me. "Oh, my gosh. This is big. Huge!"

"Well, not really." I stepped back, so she had to let me go. "She wants to do this on her own."

Tiffany shook her head. "She has no idea what she's saying right now. Believe me. You can't let her go through this alone, Cash."

"I don't want to let her go through this alone, Tiff. I want her. I want this baby. I don't know what I should do." I was lost and felt like a duck out of water.

"She's in shock," Tiffany told me. "That has to be it."

"See, I would think that too. But she was pretty freaking calm about the whole thing." I got the impression that she'd known about the pregnancy for at least a little while. "Maybe she's had some time to get used to the fact and she just doesn't want anything to do with me. Which is kind of hurtful."

Ella chewed on her bottom lip. "Yeah, but you did dump her after that trip. Maybe she thinks it's best not to marry a man who dumped her."

I had admitted to Bobbi Jo how wrong I'd been about doing that though. "What can I do to prove to her that what I did was stupid and if I could go back and change things, then I would?"

Tiffany shrugged. "Since you can't time travel, you're stuck with what happened. I know it sucks, but even I had to deal with what I'd done and do things to make it right."

"Then tell me how I can make this right." That was all I wanted to do.

Ella shook her head. "Only you will know how to make it right with the girl. You are the one who loves her."

"Oh." I put my finger to my lips. "Love. Hm."

Tiffany nodded knowingly. "They haven't said the words, Ella."

I smiled. She'd hit the nail on the head. "Yeah. We haven't said the words. And to be honest, I'm not sure I can tell her that I love her yet. We haven't gotten to know one another that well."

Ella sighed. "Then what made you think you could ask her to marry you?"

"Yeah, why did I do that?" I felt stupid for jumping the gun. "I should go talk to her."

Tiffany took my hand as I turned to leave. "Give her some space, Cash. Call or, even better, shoot her a text telling her you'd like to talk whenever she's ready. And let her know that you might've asked her to marry you a little too quickly, but that was only because of how excited you are about this baby. Share the baby first and maybe love will follow."

"Maybe you're right." I crossed my fingers as I walked out of the room.

Jasper spotted me as I came out and walked over, taking me in for a big bro-hug. "Come here, you little man, you."

"Jasper, I know you want to joke around with me, but now's not the time. I'm trying to figure out how to fix all this shit."

He let me go, popping me in the shoulder to show me he still cared. "So, now you not only need to win your girl back, you've gotta figure out how to make her marry you too. What a world, huh?"

"I've talked to the girls, and I think I'm going to chill on the marriage thing."

He nodded. "They're probably right. Talk to her and figure out what she wants, bro. Then give her whatever that is."

"I'll try." Bobbi Jo wasn't your typical girl though. "She's a lot like a man at times. I know that sounds odd, but it's true. She's honest. She doesn't try to put on airs or act like someone she's not. And I acted like I was mad at her for being that way. It was a mistake. A huge mistake."

Jasper tapped his chin as he thought. "Okay, then this might be a hell of a lot easier than I thought. If we're dealing with a woman who thinks like a man, we're half-way there. I'm a man. We're not sure what you are yet, but you're coming along nicely."

I punched him in the arm. "Can you be serious for a second, asshole. I've got a baby on the way. I would like to get my life all settled down now."

Tyrell came into the room, a beer in his hand. "I brought you this. Figured it might help you calm down a little. And ease the pain of that harsh refusal of marriage she gave you. Man, I don't know what I would do if I was dissed like that." He took a drink of the beer meant for me.

"Give me that," I barked as I took the tall, dark bottle out of his hand and chugged it. "Man, this sucks ass."

"Totally," my brothers agreed.

We all took seats as they stared at me. "So, she wants to do this all on her own. And she thinks I don't like her. But I do like her. I've messed it all up, and I've got to fix it. And I would guess that I've got about eight months to do that. So, what am I going to do?"

Jasper shook his head. "Maybe you should make her a cake."

Tyrell bumped his shoulder to Jasper's. "Or build her a house."

I looked at the idiots I had to say I was related to. "The women were much more helpful than either of you are. This is serious. I'm going to be a father. I'd like to get to actually raise my kid. Right now, that's looking like it might not happen."

"First of all," Tyrell said. "You will get to raise your kid. If Bobbi Jo wants to play hardball, you've got the harder balls. You get what I'm saying?"

I kind of understood him. "I've got balls, and she doesn't. Yeah, I know."

Jasper laughed. "You idiot. You've got enough money to get great lawyers that would make sure you get to raise your son. Bobbi Jo wouldn't have any choice in the matter."

As I sat there, chewing on that idea, I began to see things in Bobbi Jo's eyes. "Do you think she knows that about me?"

"That you can hire lawyers to get your kid?" Tyrell asked. "Um, hell yes she knows that."

"Do you think that might be a part of what has her saying she wants to do this alone?" I could understand her being worried about me being that man who takes his kid away from the woman just because he can. "She did say something about me being that typical rich man. She said she saw it in my eyes when we were on that trip."

Jasper nodded. "We all have that, Cash. I don't like it about myself, but we all have that in us. Like in our genes, man. Our grandfather passed that shit down. Dad didn't let it affect him. So, I've got faith that we can do what Dad did too. We can overcome that asshole, rich-man gene if we want to. Or we can give into it and become just like old Collin Gentry."

I never wanted to be like that man. "I won't let that happen to me. I felt it too. I felt aggravated that Bobbi Jo wouldn't like every damn thing I did for her. I ordered fancy dishes at the Waldorf, and she took one look at them and shook her head. She wouldn't even try the things. And I felt mad about her doing that. The thing is that I don't know why I felt angry about that. When I put that fucking snail into my mouth to show her how the other half lives, I nearly puked."

Jasper nodded. "I bet you did."

"I did." I'd been so stupid too. "But I chewed that nasty shit up, and I swallowed it. And then you know what I did?"

Tyrell made a gagging face. "You ran to the bathroom and then threw up?"

"No," I said as I shook my head. "I ate three more, just to prove to her that they were good. Which they were not. And then I did the same thing with the goose liver pate. I ate nearly all of it as she looked at me with disgust. Why? I don't know. And that dumbass feeling of anger at her for being true to herself just kept on going. Up until only a week or so ago, I kept thinking that she would never be what I needed in my life. You know, a woman who will do anything I want."

I heard Tiffany's voice as she and Ella came into the room to see what we were doing. "How boring would it be if a woman did everything you wanted her to?"

Tyrell nodded. "Yeah. You looking for a robot wife or what?"

"No." I wasn't looking for a wife at all—at least I hadn't been until today. "I don't know what I was thinking. But I know this. I like Bobbi Jo. I genuinely like her. And that should be enough for now."

I remembered that I'd left my cell out in the car. I jumped up to go out and get it. But I found the car was gone when I opened the front door. Tyrell was right behind me. "They already picked it up to take it to a shop in town to get it fixed."

"My phone was in it." I sagged and leaned against the wall.

Tyrell jerked his head to one side. "Go take another car to the shop to pick it up. Or better yet. Go see Bobbi Jo. She shouldn't be at work yet. And I bet she could stand to hear what you've got to say. Letting her know that you will give her the space she needs, but you will be right here, waiting for her too, ought to help."

"Yeah, it might." I looked at my big brother. "Tyrell, this is really hard for me. I'm jumping up and down inside. I'm so happy about this baby. Not getting to celebrate this with the mother of it isn't sitting well with me."

"You're a good man, Cash." Tyrell patted me on the back. "And you're going to make a great father. She'll see that. Just be yourself and let her see that she's having a baby with the right man."

"I do want to marry her." I didn't know if that was right or not, but I did want that. "But I guess I had better keep that to myself for a while, huh?"

"You might want to, yeah."

Who knew not asking her to marry me would be the best thing to do?

CHAPTER TWENTY-SIX

Bobbi Jo

My twin might've been the first person to be as close to me as any other human being could get, but now there was my little baby. I knew that person would be even closer to me. And the fact that my sister thought she knew what was best for my baby totally pissed me off.

I slammed into our house and went straight to the bedroom where I knew I would find Betty Sue. Sure enough, she was laid out on her bed, looking at her cell as if she'd done nothing wrong. "Before you say one word, Bobbi Jo, you should know I'm not the least bit sorry for what I did."

"If I weren't pregnant right now, I would do far worse to you than I did that day after you kissed Cash." My fists balled at my sides as they yearned to smack into her.

She put the cell phone down, then sat up to look at me. Not even the slightest bit of remorse was in her expression. "Why don't you take a seat, sis?"

"Why don't you jump off a bridge, sis?" I took a deep breath to try to calm myself down. "Just tell me why you would dig through the bathroom trash to find what you found."

"I was throwing it out. I found it by accident." She smiled. "And let me tell you that what I found made my heart pound and I don't remember ever feeling happier about anything. Nothing, Bobbi Jo. This is great news. Why would you want to hide it anyway?"

I sat on the chair at my desk. "There are the issues with this baby's father to consider, Betty Sue. It's not all black and white; there are a lot of gray areas. And I wanted time to consider everything before I told anyone about this baby. You took that away from me. You stole it, Betty Sue. And you're not even one tiny bit sorry for what you did."

"He deserved to know."

"Betty Sue, you didn't tell *Cash*. You told our *father*. Do you know what he did?"

She shook her head. "I had high hopes he would talk some sense into you."

"Well, your hopes are dashed then." I shook my head as I just couldn't believe how everything went down. "You should know that our father is the hottest of the hot-heads, Betty Sue. He not only pulled a gun on Cash, but he also fired it at him too."

Her eyes went wide. "You're shitting me!"

"I'm not." I put my hand on my belly, a thing I'd done since I found out about my tiny bundle of joy. "You could've gotten this baby's father killed before I even had the time to decide what I was going to do about him."

"So, what are you going to do about Cash?" she asked.

"I don't know," I said. "First of all, he doesn't like me. He doesn't like the person I am. And I will not change things about myself to suit him—or any man, for that matter. I'm okay with who I am. If he doesn't like how straightforward I am, then he doesn't have to be around me. I'm fine with that."

"But that's his baby, Bobbi Jo. He deserves to be a part of that kid's life too."

I understood that. "I never said I was going to leave him out entirely. But I'm only a little over a month pregnant. There's lots of time for me to be alone with this. But now that seems to be gone. It seems I've got to let Cash be with me, even before the baby is born. And I don't really think either of us will be happy with that. The guy thought he had to ask me to marry him. What does that say about him?"

"What does that say about you?" she asked me with a concerned expression.

"That I'm a strong woman who knows that I can have this baby on my own without anyone's help."

She shook her head. "You're delusional."

"Am not," I said. "What about all those mothers out there who have absent fathers for their kids? They do it all on their own. And they have far less resources than I do. I now own my own business. I can make my own hours, and I won't have to even worry about getting a babysitter for my baby. I can take him with me everywhere I go."

She looked upset. "So, you don't plan on even letting us help you out?"

"Who? You, Mom, and Dad?" I asked.

She nodded. "Yeah."

"Well, you can play with him, but I don't *need* you. I don't *need* any of you. Haven't I made that abundantly clear?" I didn't understand why it was so hard for everyone to grasp the fact that I had this covered.

"And what about Cash? Are you going to let *him* play with his own kid too? Or are you going to let him be the *father* he should be?" she asked.

"I don't know yet." I hadn't had time to really think about it. Cash had barely begun talking to me again. How was I to know what the future would bring?

Betty Sue seemed put out with me as she sighed and scratched her head. "Are you oblivious to all the money that man has? Are you unaware that he can get custody of that baby and leave you out of its life?"

"Well, he wouldn't do that. He's not a monster." I knew Cash better than that.

"Oh, so you know how that man will react to you not letting him see his child?" She laughed. "I think you might be underestimating how a parent can react to being kept away from their kid. It can be downright primal, Bobbi Jo. You should start thinking about the reality of this situation and stop thinking about this in your own terms. You really don't have as much power as you think you do over this baby."

"I'm the one carrying this baby. It's inside of me." I knew I had the upper hand.

"You're carrying it for now. Sure, no one can take it from you at this point. But you won't have that baby tucked safely away inside of you forever." She cocked her head to one side. "Only about eight more months is all you have. And then what will you do?"

"I haven't figured that out yet. I will. I mean, I've got to. But for now, I want to be left alone." I wasn't asking for much. I just wanted some time with my baby alone. The kid wasn't even here yet. What was the big damn deal?

A knock sounded on front door and I looked at Betty Sue as she jumped up to go answer it. "I wonder who that could be."

I followed behind her and gasped when she opened the door. Cash stood there. "How did you find out where I live?" I asked him as Betty Sue quickly disappeared.

"I stopped by the sheriff's office and your father was more than happy to give me the address." He stepped inside and closed the door behind him. "I'm not here to pressure you into anything. I want you to know that right off the bat. I feel like you need to hear me out. So, don't say a word, just listen. Okay?"

I stood there with my arms crossed, waiting.

"Okay?" he asked again.

"You said not to say anything. Can I sit down?"

He nodded. "Yeah." He took a seat in my father's recliner as I took one on the sofa. "I just wanted you to know that I'm over the moon about this baby. I felt deflated back there. I wanted to grab you and hug and kiss you. I wanted to celebrate this happy news with you.

And when you left, leaving me out, I felt like something was so wrong."

I nodded. "Yeah, I can see that. I didn't think you would be all that happy, to be honest with you."

"It's kind of surprising me too." He smiled and my heart fluttered. "Bobbi Jo, I know my actions in New York made you think I don't like you. But, honey, I do like you. I like you more than I've ever liked anyone. I think we could even fall in love, given time."

I didn't know what to say. But then I thought about the baby. "And if we never do fall in love, then what?"

"Then, we stay friends."

"The way it was before?" I asked. "Friends with benefits?"

He smiled at me. "That wasn't so bad, was it?"

It wouldn't be enough now. "Cash, I liked you too. I don't know if I do anymore. I didn't like the way you acted. For God's sakes, you ate snails and pretended you liked them."

He rubbed his brow and looked grim. "Yeah, I know I did that. I can't explain what I was trying to prove. My brothers and I talked a little about that. We have this philosophy that the genes we've inherited from our grandfather has everything to do with it when we're being assholes."

"I can see that." I couldn't help but smile. "And I can see that you will always have issues with that. And that's okay. You can't help who you are. It's just that I don't want to be a part of that."

His eyes drooped. "You don't want to be a part of me?"

I shook my head. "No, I don't."

I'd never seen that much pain in anyone's eyes before. Cash's chest even caved in as he leaned back in the chair. "Damn."

Something inside of me felt horrible that I'd made him feel that way. "Cash, don't look like that. Just because I don't want to be a part of you doesn't mean that there's not someone out there for you. There has to be some woman who wants to be what you want her to be. I'm me. I'm set in my ways. I have opinions and I don't shy away from them. I don't keep my mouth shut if I do or don't like something."

"I don't want some girl who pretends to like what I like, Bobbi Jo."

He looked at me and I saw the pain going clear to his soul. "I know I was wrong for what I thought I wanted from you. I know I was wrong for not talking to you once we got back home. And I know I'm wrong for doing this too. But I will walk away and give you all that you want: your freedom to have this baby all on your own. But I will only do that if that's what you really want."

As I sat there, listening to him give me everything I wanted and knowing he didn't want the same things, I got mad. "Cash, do you think for one second that I want you to be a person who I refuse to be? I'm not some hypocrite. And I don't like you thinking I am. You be you, okay? You say whatever you want to say, all right?"

"So you want me to do what I want to do and not to worry about how you feel about it?" he asked.

I didn't know exactly what I wanted, but I knew I didn't want him or anyone else bending to please me. Not when I wasn't about to bend to please anyone. "Be you, Cash. I'll be me, and you be you."

"Then I want to be here for you and our baby. I'll give you all the space you want, but in the end, I want to be that baby's father, and I want to be your supporter too, Bobbi Jo. I'll support you in any way you need. All you have to do is tell me what it is you need or want, and I'll do it."

"And if I say I just want to be left alone?" I asked because right then, that was all I wanted—at least for a little while.

He got up and walked to the door. "I hear you. You know where I'll be, and you've got my number. You call, text, or just show up. I want you, Bobbi Jo. I like you, Bobbi Jo. And I do believe that I could love you—given time. I think you could love me too if you want to know what I think. But I won't force anything. Well, that's not true. I will force this one thing. I *will* be that child's father. Even if I have to fight you on it; I will not walk away from my kid. I won't ever do it, and there is nothing you can do to make me. I love it already." And then he left.

I sat perfectly still, my hand on my belly. "Did you hear that? He loves you already. So do I, by the way."

Now if we can only find love for each other.

CHAPTER TWENTY-SEVEN

Cash

An entire week passed without Bobbi Jo trying to talk to me. I planned to honor the promise I made her, but something told me to do at least a little something to show her I was thinking of her.

So, my brothers and I hopped on our private jet to head to Maine. "You're going to love the lobster at Docks Boathouse." My mission was to bring back some of that delicious seafood that Bobbi Jo and I had both agreed was fantastic on the trip that had threatened to end it all.

Jasper was a little tired looking as he sprawled out in the chair. "But all the way to Maine, bro? Why so far? Can't you get some great lobster from somewhere nearer to us?"

"Nope." I looked out the window as we flew up high in the sky. "She needs this anyway. This will show her how far I'll go to do things for her; it should help her see there's no reason to shut me out."

Tyrell looked out the window on his side of the plane. "I think it's a great idea. You've got to do something. That girl is just stubborn enough to cut things off with you until she's forced to deal with you."

Jasper sat up; a smile lit up his face. "Oh, I was supposed to tell you this, and I've been forgetting. Tiffany is going to throw Bobbi Jo a surprise baby shower when she's seven months pregnant. She said that's about the official time most baby showers are thrown."

"Ella wanted to know when we could start setting up the baby's bedroom too, Cash," Tyrell said. "You've got to think about all that. No matter what, that baby needs a room in our house too."

I chewed on my lower lip as I thought about that. "I want to offer Bobbi Jo a suite in our house too. Whether she wants to be with me or not, I'd like it if we cohabitated to raise our baby."

"Then invite her to live with us," Tyrell said. "I think it's an awesome idea."

Jasper looked a little like he was on the other side of the fence. "What if you and Bobbi Jo never get back together? What if you want to date someone else? What if *she* wants to date someone else? Living in the same house, in your house, won't be a great idea."

"I don't plan on seeing anyone else." I hoped Bobbi Jo would eventually come around. "I *can* be charming, you know. I think I can win her back if she'll just allow me to be around her for a bit."

Tyrell laughed. "She's a realist, Cash. She's seen through your charming exterior and really knows who you are now."

"How can she know who I really am, when *I* don't even know who I am yet." I wasn't done growing as a person. "I'm not quite finished yet. This isn't the end result."

Jasper shrugged. "Well, what about her? What if she's not into you that way anymore?"

I laughed. "She'll be into me."

"That's a lot of guessing there. And hoping," Tyrell said. "Maybe offer to buy her a house."

"She won't let me." I knew that for a fact. "And that wouldn't help at all, anyway. I want us to be under the same roof. I want us to have equal time with our kid. And I don't want either of us to miss a single thing that goes on with that kid."

"Like waking up in the middle of the night to feed it?" Jasper asked.

I nodded. "Yeah, like that."

"You going to miraculously be able to breastfeed, little brother?" Tyrell asked with a grin.

"You know what I mean." And I had no idea if Bobbi Jo was going to breastfeed or not. "I can use a bottle even if *she* wants to breastfeed."

Jasper brought up something. "Not all moms want their baby to have a bottle in the beginning. What will you do about that?"

"I'll deal with it when it comes to it." I huffed and crossed my arms over my chest. "She's got to move in. I'll make that a stipulation or something. I want my child in my home and nowhere else."

My brothers looked at each other then they cracked up. They thought I was hilarious. But I did want my baby in my home, and Bobbi Jo would have to get on board with some of the things I wanted.

We spent the last part of the flight in silence as I mulled things over. Bobbi Jo wasn't even a whole two months pregnant yet, and already there was so much to plan for.

When we got to the restaurant, I had an epiphany. "I wonder if the chef will give me the recipe for the lobster rolls. That way I can go back with not only the food but with a recipe she can use in the grill she's opening in the bar."

Tyrell nodded. "That would be a nice gift."

So, I was going back armed with both great food and something that would make her grill stand out. I would make sure her bar and grill were both great successes.

We ate, got an ice chest full of yummy seafood for Bobbi Jo, plus the recipe, then got back on the plane. I was all psyched to see her and sent her a text, asking her if I could pick her up later and bring her to my place. I said I had a surprise for her and me. Since it was Monday, I knew she wasn't working, as she didn't open the bar on those days.

She sent me back a text telling me she'd be waiting for me. I thought that was a pretty great start. Bobbi Jo didn't often want to be without her own car to make sure she could leave whenever she wanted to.

My hopes soared high as we got back to the small municipal airport in Carthage and I put the ice chest in the backseat of my truck, then headed to Bobbi Jo's while my brothers went home. With all I had armed myself with, I felt like she would fall right into the great plans I had.

Pulling up to her parents' house, I got out of the truck and went to knock on the door. She opened it before I got a chance to knock. "I'm ready."

"Okay." I was kind of caught off guard. "You look pretty today, Bobbi Jo."

"Thanks." She headed to the truck, going to the passenger side.

It was a good ways up to the seat, and there wasn't a step to help her get up. So I walked up behind her as she hopped a couple of times to get herself up into the seat. Placing my hands on either side of her waist, I lifted her. "Here you go."

"Thanks." She closed the door quickly after I helped her up. After I got in, she looked at the ice chest in the backseat, then at me. "Where have you been today?"

"Maine," I said with a grin. "I went to go get you something I knew you would never go and get yourself."

She sighed as she gripped her hands in her lap. "That was thoughtful of you."

"I've done nothing but think about you, Bobbi Jo." I thought I should bring up the fact that she hadn't gotten in touch with me the whole week. "I've missed hearing your voice this last week."

"Oh."

I figured she was just moody with hormones. "Well, how was your week, Bobbi Jo?"

"Full." She sighed heavily. "The health department doesn't want to give me a permit until I make some huge changes to the bar. I called a contractor to see how much the changes would cost me and it's more than what I have. So, I guess the grill part is out."

"It doesn't have to be." I was still willing to go into a partnership with her. "Whether we ever planned on this or not, we're going to be parents together. We might as well be business partners too. We can make that whole bar over if you want to."

She looked out of the corner of her eye at me. "If you did want to come in as a partner, I could only let you put in the same amount of money as I have in it. That would be what the bar is currently worth, plus the money I've got in the bank. I couldn't let you do any more than that. And to make the addition to the structure, plus put in the professional grill, the cost is over three hundred thousand dollars. It's not doable."

"All I see is that some contractor is feeding you a line of shit." I knew that couldn't be right. "I'll find one who will be reasonable. We'll get that grill going, don't you worry. And I've even got a couple of recipes for you to start with. The lobster rolls, for one." I handed her my phone where I put the recipe in my notes. "The chef gave me the recipe and the right to use it. And for the other, we can serve small chunks of steak; we can call them Whisper Bites. The meat for the grill can come from our cattle. We'll make sure to put cattle for the grill in a grass pasture so they'll be only grass fed. That's a thing people like nowadays."

"You've sure been thinking about my business a lot." She turned her head to look at me. "*My* business, Cash."

I nodded. "Am I overstepping my bounds here, Bobbi Jo?"

"You might be. When I tell you what I've got to tell you, you might just want to take your offers back." She ducked her head and wrung her hands in her lap.

I decided to make her feel a hell of a lot more comfortable. "Baby, I don't want to take anything back. As a matter of fact, I want you to know that I want you to live at the ranch too. I want to give you your very own suite. We can make the baby's room right in between ours. And maybe, one day, you'll decide to move into my room, if we ever find ourselves wanting to be romantic again."

"You may not want that at all, Cash." She started to cry, and I pulled the truck over.

"Bobbi Jo, what's wrong?"

She shook her head and kept crying. And I only had one thing on my mind.

Is the baby all right?

CHAPTER TWENTY-EIGHT

Bobbi Jo

The morning hadn't gone very well. I kept trying to tell myself that whatever happened was meant to happen. But it wasn't helping me much. No matter how many times I told myself that, it still hurt.

Cash had pulled the truck over; his expression was one of compassion as he asked, "Bobbi Jo, what's wrong?"

I wasn't sure how to say it. And the sobs that had erupted stopped me from being able to say a word. "I ..." That was all I got out before a lump got stuck in my throat.

He took off his seatbelt, then slid over to me. His strong arms around me felt good. I buried my face in his chest as he shushed me. "Baby, come on now. You can tell me what's wrong."

Just having him hold me that way had me feeling better. But only a little. "Cash, I'm not sure if I'm still pregnant. I woke up this morning and there was some blood in my panties. When I went to the restroom, there was a little more. I didn't have a pregnancy test at home to take. We may not be having a baby at all. I might've lost it. Or at least be losing it. It's so tiny right now. That's why I didn't even want to tell anyone. I wanted to wait until I was three or four months pregnant before I said anything."

"We're going to the emergency room right now." He kissed me on top of my head. "You just sit back and don't worry about a damn thing."

"I don't think this is considered an emergency, Cash." I tried to stop crying and opened the glovebox to see if I could find something to dry my tears and blow my nose with.

"It's an emergency to me." He reached into the compartment of his door, then handed me some napkins. "Here you go."

"Thanks." I blew my nose, then wiped my eyes. "Cash, if I'm not pregnant, I don't expect you to stand up to what you've just said."

"I *want* to be your partner." He looked at me as he took a left to go toward the hospital. "And I *want* to see you, Bobbi Jo. I like you. I want you. I don't care if you're carrying my baby or not. I want you."

"Really?" I found that hard to believe. "After how I've kept to myself and not given you any chances? You still want to see me?"

"I do." He reached out and took my hand. "The one thing I've found out about this is that I miss you every single day. I don't want to keep on missing you. I want you with me. I want you with me every day."

Before our breakup, he had come to the bar each night to hang out with me, even when it didn't end up in having sex. "You mean that?"

He nodded. "I mean it. I enjoy your company. And I really meant the apologies I've made to you. And if you will recall, I made them before I knew you were pregnant. This isn't all because of the baby. This is because I want you. And you know what else I can say and mean it?"

"No." I was still reeling from the fact that he wanted to see me even if I wasn't pregnant.

"I went to Maine for you. I can't stop thinking about you. And that means something to me." He squeezed my hand. "It means I love you, Bobbi Jo Baker."

I closed my eyes as I took in his words. "You love me."

"I love you." He pulled up in the parking lot of the emergency room, clicked the tab to release the seatbelt, then pulled me to his side. "Please tell me that no matter what happens with this baby, that you won't keep yourself from me. I don't think I'm the best man I can be if I don't have you. You make me want to be a better man, Bobbi Jo."

My breath caught in my throat. I had no idea what to say at all. And then it slipped out of my mouth. "I love you too, Cash."

The smile he wore went all the way to his eyes. His lips pressed against mine and I felt like the weight of the world had lifted off my shoulders. I'd felt so heavy for so long. Now it was all gone.

He pulled his mouth off mine. "Let's go inside and see what's happening."

So, we got out, went in, and found out that I was still pregnant. The doctor said spotting happened sometimes, and it might even happen more. As long as it wasn't a lot and no cramps accompanied it, then I was fine.

We left knowing we were still having a baby and now, we were in love too. Cash stopped just before lifting me back into his truck. "Don't answer me right now. But one day, I will marry you, Bobbi Jo Baker. I'm going to take you home now. To *our* home."

"Wait." I wasn't ready to do all that. "I want my independence. Living with you will take that all away. I still want to know that I can do this on my own."

His jaw tight, his body tense, he stared at me. "Bobbi Jo, why do you want to make this so hard on yourself?"

"Because I want to know I can handle it." I put my foot down.

"But I'm here and I can help." He didn't seem to be backing down at all.

"Do you love me?" I asked him as I crossed my arms over my chest.

"I do." He put his hands on my shoulders. "And all I want to do is take you home, put your sweet little ass into my bed—a bed that is soon to be known as *ours*—and make sweet love to you."

And that sounded pretty great to me too. "Okay. Let's do that. But then I'll go home. I want to get my own place. I want to go through this alone."

His jaw set, his body tensed up again; he could only stare at me. "You've got to be kidding me. You've got a man with tons of money and you want to do this on your own. You don't make any sense."

"Cash, I've got to know that I can do this without anyone's help."

He picked me up and put me in the truck. "Scoot over. We'll talk about this afterward."

"After what?" I asked as I scooted over, then he slid in behind the wheel.

"After I take you home and we connect in a way that I've only ever connected with you before." He started the truck and off we went. He draped his arm around me, then kissed the side of my head. "I think you need to be reminded of how good we are together. Afterward, if you still want to be all alone, then we'll talk. I want you in my bed or just down the hallway. And I want our baby in our home too. I want to share everything with you."

"Then you'll expect me to share everything with you too." I wasn't sure if I wanted to do that.

"Sharing is what people who love each other do, Bobbi Jo." He wasn't giving up.

And for a moment, I was okay with that. I shut my mouth and rested my head on his shoulder. "Maybe we should have sex. Maybe that would help me make decisions."

"And maybe you might decide to take a backseat and let me make some decisions too." He kissed the side of my head. "I am going to be the head of our family, Bobbi Jo."

I had to laugh. "You had better take a step or two back, big daddy. Little momma here has something to say about how things go too."

He laughed then kissed my cheek. "I'm just messin' with ya, babe. When it comes to our kid and us, we'll make decisions together."

As we rode out to the ranch, I really looked at the scenery as we passed by it. Tall oaks, old mesquite trees, and even some maple trees lined the road. Our kid would call this place home. Our kid would see this road on his way home to the ranch he would grow up on. And nothing could've ever made me happier.

"You know what, Cash?" I asked as we pulled up to the driveway. "We should be business partners too. I really like the idea you had about grass-fed beef. And we could do free-range chickens too. We could even make a big garden so we could have organically grown vegetables." I was getting all kinds of excited.

"Should we change the name of it too?" he asked me. "You know, to incorporate us and the ranch?"

"What if we call it, Whisper Bar and Grill?" I liked the sound of that. "That way the ranch will be known for more than just racehorse semen. I'd like my kids to have a better reputation than just semen ranchers."

"Kids?" he asked, laughing. "More than one?"

"Well, you'll have to marry me if you want to make more kids. I'm done giving you babies out of wedlock. I do have a reputation to uphold, you know. I don't want to be the only one in our little family who doesn't carry the last name of Gentry."

"I hope you brought a ring with you, baby." He pulled up in front of the wood cabin mansion that would be my new home. Then he reached into his pocket and pulled out a huge diamond ring. "But if you don't, that's okay. I happen to have something that will do for now."

I looked at the ring then at him. "Cash Gentry, will you do me the great honor of becoming my husband?"

He smiled. "I will. And Bobbi Jo Baker, will you do me the great honor of becoming my wife?"

"I will." I kissed the man I knew I would struggle with, have tons of fun with, and share all my love with.

Until death do us part.

CHAPTER TWENTY-NINE

Cash

Seven months pregnant and the baby shower had begun. My parents had come, as we had the party at a hotel in Dallas. Bobbi Jo's parents and mine were meeting for the first time.

She and I had run off to Vegas to tie the knot after agreeing to get married. We didn't want to wait long to get married and change her name to mine.

As our parents talked quietly in a corner, Bobbi Jo and I sat together as her sister opened the presents. Bobbi Jo hadn't been feeling well in the last week. She had an appointment in a week, so we decided it wasn't anything she needed to make a special appointment about. Until she gasped for air, grabbed my hand, then looked at me with frightened eyes. "Cash!"

"What's wrong?" I looked into her eyes and found pure panic in them.

"Something's wrong." She leaned into me and I felt heat coming off her.

"With the baby?" I asked as everyone gathered around us.

"I don't think so. I think it's just me." She took a shallow breath. "I think you need to get me to a hospital."

When I got up and pulled her to get up too, she collapsed. I caught her just in time, then carried her out.

"You should call an ambulance!" her father shouted.

"I can get her there faster than waiting on them." I got down to the lobby with her in my arms. She'd passed out, but I could tell she was still breathing.

Tyrell hurried to get the valet to bring his car around then we got into the back, and he drove us to the closest hospital. All I could do was keep kissing her on top of the head and praying that everything would be okay. "You're going to be all right. This is just a cold or something." It had to be something that easy; it just had to.

An hour later, with Bobbi Jo in a bed in the emergency room, the attending physician came in with a grim look on her face. "We've got the lab results back. And by what I see here, we're going to have to admit her. Her white blood cell count is very high."

Bobbi Jo looked up at me with frightened eyes. "What does that mean?"

I shook my head. "I don't know."

The doctor added, "We don't know either until we can get more tests done. Bobbi Jo, is there anything that's been happening to your body that's out of the ordinary?"

She chewed on her lower lip. "Well, I don't know if this is out of the ordinary or not for a pregnancy."

The doctor nodded. "Just tell me what it is."

"My left breast has been hurting. And some discharge has been leaking out of it. It smells bad too." Bobbi Jo looked up at me. "It started about five days ago. I didn't say anything to you because I thought it was normal."

I had to hold my tongue, pissed that she'd kept it to herself. "Well, we're here now. We can see if you need some help." I took her hand and held it up to my lips. "But, baby, you really should've told me when it first happened. You wouldn't have gone through so much pain, and this never would've happened if you had just told me."

The doctor nodded, agreeing, "It's important to let your husband know if anything is happening to you, Bobbi Jo. Where your health is concerned, you should always reach out for help."

Bobbi Jo nodded. "Yeah, I can see that now."

An hour later, we were in a private hospital room—along with our parents—when another doctor came in. "I'm Dr. Harvey. I've been brought in to see you. The lab results have been sent to my office and what I saw bothered me. If I could do an examination, that might help us to get to the bottom of things."

I nodded, and our parents left the room as the doctor pulled the hospital gown back to examine Bobbi Jo's left breast. She winced with pain as he pressed on her breast only slightly. And with that small amount of force, a dark liquid came out of her nipple.

He didn't have to say a word. I knew what was going on instinctively. "It's cancer, isn't it?"

"I'm afraid so." The doctor covered Bobbi Jo's breast then looked at me as my wife cried quietly. "We should operate immediately. And then we'll have to do radiation and maybe even chemo."

"No," Bobbi Jo whimpered. "I won't do anything until I have the baby. I won't put poison in my baby's system."

I sat down next to her, holding her hand, trying so hard not to cry myself. "Bobbi Jo, we've got to get you through this. *You're* important here too. Let's hear what the doctor has to say."

"No." She looked at me through the tears. "I won't do anything until the baby is born."

The doctor interjected. "Look, we've got more testing to do. I've ordered an MRI to get to the bottom of everything that is affected by this cancer. We can make decisions after we know more."

Bobbi Jo was being her usual stubborn self as she said, "It doesn't matter. My baby comes first."

The doctor reminded her of an important fact, "Don't you want to be around to see that baby, Bobbi Jo? Cancer moves fast. And the fact that you are pregnant with so many hormones moving through your body is only making this cancer grow even faster. You've got a chance to make it through this. Once it spreads to your lymph nodes, you lose some of the chances you have right now."

"No," she said again.

I hugged her. "Let them do what they need to do, baby."

"No," she whispered. "I won't let them do anything until the baby is born."

I didn't know what to do. I let her go and got up, leaving the room. She'd always been headstrong. But would she die before doing what someone else thought was best for her?

What could I do? Could I make her do what the doctors thought best? Could I demand that they do what I say and ignore her? Where did I stand on this? What rights did I have?

My wife wanted to sit there and do nothing for two months while cancer ravaged her body. And she expected me to sit by and let that happen?

No.

Hell no!

I went back into her room to find the doctor gone and her staring vacantly out the window. "I know you're mad at me, Cash. I can't help that. If I can hold onto this baby for another couple of weeks, then he's got a fighting chance. If I go under the knife, under the anesthesia, then there's a risk that I will die on the operating table. And our son will die with me."

"You don't know that." I hated when she thought she knew something and she really didn't. "You were so sure you were going to have a girl and you were wrong about that. What about that, Bobbi Jo? You're not always right." I didn't want to go into the whole thing, but she'd already begun the thought process, so I had to step into it too. "And if you did die on the table, the baby might not. He might be saved and then what? You're going to leave me alone to take care of a baby who's born two months early. And then you expect me to raise this boy all alone too. Well, no, Bobbi Jo. I want you with me."

She turned her head to face me. The tears had stained her cheeks. "You're Sway's father. You will have to take care of him no matter what. I told you I wanted to do this on my own and God took that out of my hands. But he put it into yours. You may have to do this alone, Cash. It might just have to be that way. But I will not go under the knife and make those chances any greater. I won't do it, so don't ask me to."

I had no idea what to say anymore. But there wasn't anything she could do about assessing the severity of her situation. After the MRI results came in, another doctor came into her room. The expression he wore told me the news wasn't good at all.

"Hey, doc," I said quietly as Bobbi Jo lay in the bed, not speaking, not blinking, not doing a damn thing. "What's going on with my wife?"

He looked at my wife. "You have been in pain for some time, haven't you?"

She didn't nod or say a word. And I couldn't believe she would do this to us. "Bobbi Jo, what have you done?"

The doctor pulled something out of the large envelope he held. "This is the tumor in your wife's left breast." He handed the thing to me. "And all those little circles under her left arm are where the cancer has taken over her lymph nodes. She's known something was wrong for about almost two months. Isn't that right, Mrs. Gentry?"

Bobbi Jo still didn't move or she say a single word in her defense. And I knew she had known something was wrong and she just hadn't told me or even her doctor.

"Is there anything we can do?" I asked him.

"We need to get her into surgery and we need to do it quickly," he said.

"I won't do it until I have the baby. That's why I didn't say anything when I first felt the pain and saw the discharge." Bobbi Jo looked at me with tired eyes. "I'm sorry. I really am. But I won't ever put the baby's life in jeopardy. His life is more important than mine."

I fell to my knees beside the bed. I held her hand and couldn't hold the tears back anymore. "Don't even say that. Please, Bobbi Jo. I love you. I don't want to lose you. I love our baby too, and he's got a chance here." I looked at the doctor. "Get me an obstetrician in here, please. I need to find some things out."

He nodded then left us alone. Bobbi Jo looked away from me again. "I don't know what you think can be done, Cash. I've thought this through. I've looked things up about this. I'll have to wait until the baby can be born safely. I won't agree to do anything else."

"I love you. I want you to keep on remembering that when things happen." I wasn't going to lose either of them. I wouldn't be able to live without either of them.

I won't live without either of them.

CHAPTER THIRTY

Bobbi Jo

As my mother and father sat on either side of me, I tried to put on a brave face even as I fell apart inside. "It's going to be okay. You'll see. I'm going to have the baby in a month or so, and after he's born, I'll deal with the cancer."

Cash had left the room so I could talk to my parents. He'd said something about needing to get some facts straight. I knew he was grasping at straws, but I had to let him do something so he didn't feel useless.

Dad got up, wiping his hand over his face. "Bobbi Jo, I don't like this. You've been in pain and haven't told a single soul. Not even your husband. Girl, this isn't right."

Mom ran her hand over my forehead. "You should've told him, honey."

"Why?" I knew what he would've done. "I was only five months pregnant when I felt the first pain. If I would've told him then, he would've made me go to the doctor and stayed on me until I did whatever they wanted me to do. And we would've lost our son."

Mom sighed. "Sweetheart, more children can come to you. But

you've got to be alive for that to happen. And Cash would've been right to make you get medical help. And that's why we're behind him with what he's trying to get you to do now."

"I know he means well, but this is *my* body. I want to wait." I knew I could make it long enough to have my baby.

My sister came into my room, her face red, her eyes swollen from crying. "Why, Bobbi Jo? Why did you do this to yourself? I hate you for this. I really do." She fell on her knees, shaking her hands in the air. "Why did you not let me feel her pain this time?"

"I'm glad you can't feel it, Betty Sue. I wouldn't wish this on anyone." I had no idea how much pain a person could live through. I was finding that out though.

Cash came in; a couple of doctors were right behind him. "I've figured it all out, Bobbi Jo. And you're going to like this." He stepped to the side as the doctors came around him. "Tell her what you can do."

"I'm Dr. Janice Prince," the woman introduced herself. "I am a specialist in premature babies. I will be personally taking care of little Sway when he is born."

The man introduced himself. "I am Doctor John Friedman. I am an OB-GYN. We've talked to the oncologist on your case."

I didn't care to hear what they had to say. "Look, I know you mean well, but I've made my decision."

Cash was suddenly at my side, his hand on my shoulder. "Hear them out, Bobbi Jo."

"But I don't—" I had to shut my mouth as my daddy put his hand on my other shoulder.

"Bobbi Jo, you hush up and listen now." He patted my shoulder. "We all love you, and we all love that baby you're carrying. Now, you let these nice doctors tell us all what can be done to help you both. And you just sit back and let us take the reins here, girl. Between your momma, your daddy, and your husband, I think you should feel like you're in good hands."

Betty Sue wiped her eyes and sniffled. "Don't forget about me. You've got your twin sister here too. You know I'm not about to let them do anything to hurt that baby. I can't wait to meet baby Sway."

Looking at all the caring eyes around me, I felt like I had no choice. "I'm not making any promises, but I will hear what you've got to say, doctors."

"Good," Dr, Prince said. "See, we can take this baby by C-section. We can deliver him safely at this time. With the MRI results, we were able to see that everything is looking good with your baby boy. And my team and I will be ready to deal with anything that might happen after the delivery. I can assure you that we have had to deal with worse situations, my dear."

Dr. Friedman took over. "I can have this baby delivered within an hour. With you already under anesthesia, your oncologist will be able to work with the surgeon to do whatever it takes to get you on the road to recovery. And you will go into that knowing your baby is safely out of your womb. That has been your primary concern, has it not?"

I had to nod. "Yeah." I looked at Cash. "You really think this is a good idea?"

He laughed as he looked at everyone else in the room. "I sure do."

"I don't know." I felt like things were moving too fast.

Cash kissed my cheek, then whispered, "*I* do know. Let me make this decision for us. For all of us—*our* family, Bobbi Jo. Like we agreed in our wedding vows, sometimes you would make the big decisions and sometimes I would. It's my turn now. Let me make this decision that affects our family."

"I might not be much help if I'm undergoing all this surgery and chemo and stuff." I knew I would be useless. "Can you handle the baby on your own?"

"If I have to, I will." He looked at my family. "But I think between your family and mine, I'll have all the help I need."

"You bet you will," Dad said. "Let him make this decision, Bobbi Jo. Trust the man. He won't steer you wrong. This man loves you and that baby."

I looked back at Cash. "You do love us, don't you?"

"More than anything else in this entire world." He kissed my lips softly. "So, can you sign the papers and put me in charge of your body for a while? I swear to you that I will only make good decisions where you're concerned."

I took his hand, pulling him close so I could tell him something I didn't want anyone else to hear me say. I didn't need that kind of hassle. "Cash, if my heart gives out while they're working on me, I want you to let me go. I want you to let me die."

He only shook his head. "No way in hell, Mrs. Gentry. I will have them bring you back to me and Sway over and over. So be ready to fight to live. I'll be fighting for that too."

"Well, damn." I didn't know what else to do. "You really do love me, don't you?"

He nodded. "I really do."

I looked at the doctors. "Okay, give me the papers to sign, and I'll put my life in my husband's hands."

After signing the papers, I looked up and talked straight to God. "I sure hope you know what you're doing up there, Lord."

Cash kissed me again. "Don't worry; He does."

As I looked into my husband's eyes, I tried hard not to cry but failed miserably.

Damn, I've got no strength left at all.

EPILOGUE

Cash

S itting in a rocker in my wife's hospital room, I waited for them to bring her in. "She'll be here soon, Sway. She's out of surgery and is waking up now. That's what they told me. And soon you'll get to meet her face to face. She's very beautiful, so don't be alarmed. And don't worry about it when she cries when she sees you. You're pretty damn adorable yourself. But with a mom like Bobbi Jo, what could you expect, right?"

The door opened, and a whole bed came into the room. "Here she is," a nurse whispered as they brought my wife in. "She's awake, her throat's a little sore, and she's kind of loopy still from the medication. You'll have to hold the baby for her, Mr. Gentry. Don't think she can hold him on her own. That's going to be a while."

"Yeah, I know." I got up, holding my tiny son to my chest. "Can you believe he weighs three pounds?" I looked into Bobbi Jo's eyes. "You ate like a horse for the most part. You would've thought our son would've had some more meat on his bones."

"Sorry," she said with a scratchy voice.

The nurses backed away, leaving us alone. I put our son on the right side of my wife so she could look at him. "Take him all in. He's a keeper, baby."

She nodded as tears filled her eyes. "He's got your hair."

"Yeah." I kissed the top of her blonde head. "Maybe the next one will have your hair."

She looked up at me with big, glassy eyes. "No more."

I only laughed. "We'll see. So, you made it through surgery all right. I knew you would."

"But there's more," she said as she looked back at Sway.

"There is," I agreed. "But you can do it. You've got this little guy to make sure you do. And plus, you love me too. You've got a lot to live for."

She nodded. "Yeah." She ran her right hand over our baby's tiny head. "He's so small."

"He'll be big before you know it." I sat on the right side of her bed. "We'll be looking back at this day and wishing he was still this little. Of course, he'll be swinging from the chandeliers then and we'll be kind of mad at him for doing it."

She shook her head. "No, he won't."

I had my doubts. "Well, maybe he'll be a good boy. You'll have to get better to make sure that happens. I might spoil him rotten if you leave it all up to me."

She smiled. "I guess I'll have to try very hard not to let this cancer kill me, huh? I can't have you spoiling our boy."

"You better try very hard, Mrs. Gentry." I had so many plans for us; she had to stick around so they could come true. "First of all, while you were out and I was in charge, I made an executive decision."

Her eyes rolled. "What is it?"

"You're going to stay home for at least the first year. I've put your sister in charge of the bar and grill." I smiled at her because Bobbi Jo had been grooming her sister to fill in for us while we had the baby anyway.

"Good." She ran her hand over my cheek. "I want to stay home with you and Sway for a long time anyway."

"I want that too." I had no idea when I would be able to let my wife be away from me for any real length of time again. The time she was in surgery was miserable. I didn't know how much more I could take. "I want you right with me as much as I can have you."

"Me too." She leaned her head against me as we looked at our baby, tears in both our eyes.

The sun began to set outside the hospital window and night would soon be upon us. My little family might be starting out on shaky ground, but I had the faith that soon we'd be back at the ranch. One day soon, life wouldn't be like this, so unstable. One day we'd all be laughing again. One day, we'd look back at this time and thank God for all he'd done for us.

It might be at the beginning of our lives as a family, but I knew we'd found what everyone was looking for.

We'd found our happily ever after.

The End

COPYRIGHT

Lightning Source UK Ltd.
Milton Keynes UK
UKHW020125200221
379098UK00003B/298